Legacy of a Magical Cottage

Legacy of a Magical Cottage

SEQUEL TO
THE MAGICAL STONE COTTAGE

Shirley Cochran

To order additional copies of this book, contact:
Xlibris Corporation
1-888-795-4274
www.Xlibris.com
Orders@Xlibris.com
36025

Chapter 1

Roberta grew up in what most people would consider a very strange environment. Her father Robert and brother Francis were able to see the world of spirits, elementals, angels, and those who had passed over. Her mother Anna, who had died when Roberta was just over a week old, had the gift of being able to see this other world and had been quite famous for her paintings. Her mother Anna also could sense disease in people and could direct energy through her hands to heal, and Francis had this ability from a young age. While her father did not have the ability to heal that her mother and Francis had, he was very interested in the study of plants and herbs and used these to heal. They all lived at a healing center that her father and mother had built on their property and Robert and Francis worked here with many of their friends.

Roberta did not have any of these abilities, and, although she loved her father and brother very much, she often felt uncomfortable with them and some of the others who worked at the center. She was more comfortable with her mother's Aunt Helen and Uncle Ted. Aunt Helen and Uncle Ted had moved from town when he retired shortly after her mother died in order to help her father care for her and Francis, and they lived in a small cabin next to the house she shared with her father and Francis.

Aunt Lilith, who was actually only a close family friend, had moved from town to live in one of the cabins up by the center when Roberta was about three years old. Lilith and her mother had been very close friends, and Roberta loved to curl up and listen to Lilith talk about when her mother was learning to paint and when she had fallen in love with her father. Her mother had done paintings of everyone, even Roberta's sister Diana who had died very young, but there were no pictures of her mother, and she would have Lilith describe her mother over and over in an effort to get a clear picture of her.

Roberta also enjoyed hanging around the center and playing with the children of the people who ran the center and lived in cabins behind it. Patrick and Laura and Brian and Noreen had worked for her mother before the center had been built and were more like members of the family than employees. Everyone who lived or worked at the center gathered each evening in the large meeting room for dinner and to discuss the day's problems and future plans. Roberta loved these evenings with everyone talking and playing music and singing after dinner and then walking home with her father, Francis, Uncle Ted and Aunt Helen in the gathering darkness. Others who worked at the center as healers or counselors and even guests who were staying in one of the cabins while they underwent treatment for an illness often joined them for dinner. Fruits and vegetables were grown on the property, and there were chickens, so there was an abundance of fresh eggs, fruits and vegetables. Laura and Noreen, along with the other staff, spent their days preparing food in the kitchen at the center for meals and for use in the winter or to sell.

On Saturdays the center was very busy, and they always hired someone to play music. This was Roberta's favorite day because she loved music and would sit for hours listening as the people played different instruments and sometimes sang. One day, the summer before Roberta was to start school, a woman came who played a wooden indian flute. Roberta had heard others play flutes, but it had never sounded like this, and she asked her father that night at dinner if she could have a flute like the one the woman had played. Robert agreed to get her a flute but then forgot about it until later that evening when he was sitting on the porch and Anna appeared and urged him to get the flute for Roberta because this was important to her purpose in life. The following day, Robert contacted the flutist requesting her help in getting Roberta a flute.

It seemed to Roberta that an eternity passed before the flute finally arrived, but finally it did and she hurriedly unwrapped the package and took it with her to sit beside a secluded pool at the back of the property. She experimented with different notes and by the time that her father came to find her for dinner she was doing quite well combining notes to form harmonious sounds. He stood for a while watching as she sat with her eyes closed unaware of the elementals that danced around her and the fairies that flew overhead. When she stopped to take a breath, he stepped into the clearing and quietly told her it was time to go to the center for dinner. As they walked together through the lengthening early evening shadows, Roberta talked about seeing different colors when she closed her eyes and played, and Robert told her about the elementals that had been dancing around her.

Each day Roberta would grab her flute immediately after breakfast and could often be seen dancing across the meadow and under the trees with her eyes closed playing music that seemed to come from a place deep within. Although she had no musical training, her music was very hauntingly uplifting and soothing.

About a month after she got the flute, her father asked if she would like to play at the center one Saturday because the person who had been scheduled to play was sick. Roberta hesitated because she had never played for others before except occasionally at the center after dinner for the family, but she agreed. She was at the center early because she was so nervous, but as usual when she closed her eyes and started to play she became unaware of everyone and everything around her. The more she played, the more she felt the music vibrating within her body, and she seemed to be transported to a world of swirling lights where she floated carried high by the vibration of the notes. She played like this for a couple of hours and then let the sounds fade and slowly opened her eyes. She seemed to be dazed, and Robert led her by the arm to the kitchen where they sat down to have a glass of lemonade and take a break. He told her that she had played beautifully and listened as she talked excitedly about what she had experienced. After a short break, she hurried back to play some more, and Robert stood watching as the hazy figure of her mother bent and kissed her gently on the cheek. He smiled as Roberta brushed at her cheek in annoyance and continued to play her flute unaware what had happened.

Life at the center was peaceful and happy until the day that Roberta was to start school and was told that she could not take her flute. She sat down, crossed her arms and stated that if she couldn't take the flute, she just wouldn't go to school. It took all of them to finally convince her that she had to go to school and couldn't take the flute, and by that time she had missed the first day. The following morning her father steeled himself for a fight, but Roberta was resigned and gave him a kiss on the cheek when he left her at school. She had never been around many people other than those at the center, and she was shocked at how mean and selfish some of the other children were. When she got home that afternoon she announced that she didn't like those people at all, and she just wasn't going back. This time Robert knew that he had to be firm, and he very sternly told her that everyone had to go to school and that in life it is sometimes necessary to do things that we really don't want to do. Roberta went to her room with tears pouring down her cheeks wondering what she had done to make her father stop loving her.

When Robert dropped her at school the next day, his heart broke at the sight of her tiny shoulders drooping in dejection, and it was all he could do not to take her back home. She was still subdued that afternoon when she got home from school, and he took her to sit beside the pool where he explained to her about how rules are necessary in order for groups of people to live together. She talked about how hateful some of the children were, and he explained that not everyone had been raised with love the way she had and that some people only know hate in their lives. He told her we should try not judge others because we don't know the circumstances of their lives. They both felt better as they walked back to the center for dinner, and she placed her small hand trustingly in his as she skipped along beside him. He looked ahead on the path and saw Anna and their other daughter Diana appear and smile approvingly before slowly fading away.

Roberta soon adapted to school and even made a couple of friends. She had a very curious mind and found that she enjoyed learning but often became bored with the plodding pace. She always wanted to know more details, but all they were given were dull facts, and when she asked questions she was told that she didn't need to know more than what she was being taught. She had always been encouraged to ask questions at home, and she couldn't understand why the teacher got so upset because she asked questions at school where she was supposed to be learning. As the school year dragged on, she longed for the Christmas Holiday when she would be free to play her flute and be with people who were loving, kind and patient and who were always willing to answer her questions.

Christmas vacation finally arrived and Roberta's spirits soared as she was caught up in the excitement and secrecy of buying and wrapping gifts and preparing for the big day. Tables were set up in the large meeting room and the atmosphere was festive as everyone pitched in to prepare the special dinner. Christmas Day was a wonderful affair at the center with beautiful decorations, gifts piled under the tree and a long table groaning under the weight of every imaginable food and dessert. After dinner there was music and singing as everyone celebrated the season and talked about the true meaning of the celebration as they exchanged gifts. The evening ended with a prayer for world peace, help for all those who were in need and gratitude for the many blessings bestowed on those present. Roberta, her father, brother, aunt and uncle walked home from the center huddled in their coats against the cold, enjoying the beauty of the landscape that sparkled like diamonds under a clear sky filled with stars and a bright moon. It had been a long day, and Roberta snuggled into her bed where she promptly fell asleep and dreamed of a magical world made of beautiful crystals in every color and people who shined with a brilliant light from within and floated through the air.

The vacation time passed quickly, and it seemed only a couple of days before it was time to return to school. She had talked to her father about the problem with asking questions, and he told her to just wait until she got home, and he would try to answer her questions. It upset him to think that the very people who were responsible for teaching her would quell her natural curiosity and thirst for knowledge.

Chapter 2

Roberta grew quite close to one girl in her class that no one else wanted to be friends with because her clothes were always dirty, and she often smelled bad. The girl, whose name was Judy, was very quiet and never talked about her family but listened raptly when Roberta talked about her life and home. She was always very nervous and jumped if surprised. She came to school one day with bruises on her arms and acted as though it hurt when she moved. Roberta tried to find out what had happened, but Judy became very nervous when she asked questions and started to cry. Judy appeared to be terrified and refused to discuss it at all. As soon as Roberta got home, she sought out her father and told him she had to talk to him. Robert could tell that something was wrong and stopped what he was doing to give her his attention as Roberta described how Judy's arms looked and how she acted like it hurt when she moved. That night at dinner, Robert told everyone what Roberta had told him about Judy and after they had questioned Roberta more, it was agreed that something should be done to help her friend. Lilith had been a very successful businesswoman and said she would contact some people she knew for help with this.

The following day a woman came to school and took Judy away. Roberta didn't know what had happened, and she went straight to Lilith's cabin when she got home. Lilith explained that the police had gone to Judy's home and arrested her father and mother after they found a younger boy in very bad shape. Judy's brother had been taken to the hospital, and Judy had been taken to a doctor to make certain she didn't have any serious injuries because she had apparently been very badly beaten. Roberta begged Lilith to do something so that Judy could come stay with them, and after talking it over at dinner they all agreed it would be good for the children to come to live with them at the center. Lilith said she would use her contacts to try to have both children placed in her care, and of course everyone promised to help care for them.

Judy wasn't at school the following day, and Roberta was relieved when she got home to find a clean, well-dressed Judy waiting impatiently for her. Roberta took Judy to the pool where they talked about all that had happened, and then after a while when Judy seemed to become tired and sad Roberta took out her flute and played. Judy had never heard music like this and she began to cry, as the music seemed to reach within her and bring to the surface the pain and suffering she had undergone in her young life. Roberta stopped playing and putting her arms around her friend patted her back until she stopped crying. That night Judy asked if she could sleep with Roberta, and Robert and Lilith both agreed that this would probably be best since everything was strange here.

The next morning Judy and Roberta went to school together. One of the boys started to tease Judy about being clean and having new clothes, but Roberta stepped toward him, and he took one look at her face and walked away. A week later Judy's little brother Henry was able to leave the hospital and join her at the center. Francis had always wanted a brother, and he asked for Henry to share his room since Judy shared a room with Roberta. Francis was able to feel where the physical and emotional scars were in Henry and worked slowly to help him heal. It was months before the little boy showed anything except fear when approached by others, but he slowly came to know what it was to be loved and finally the day came when he laughed for the first time. Two new people in the tiny house had certainly caused it to be crowded, so after a week the men had begun the work of adding another room.

Roberta continued to play her flute and even occasionally played around with the piano in the center, but the piano didn't give her the same feeling that playing the flute did. When Roberta was 10 years old a woman brought her harp to the center to play, and Roberta spent the entire day listening to her play and watching the way her hands moved over the strings. She had heard others play the harp but it had never moved her the way this did. The harpist stopped to take a break after a couple of hours and Roberta approached to ask if she could touch the harp. The woman hesitated but then agreed as she saw the longing in the young eyes. She watched as Roberta sat down and carefully drew the harp against her tiny shoulder. She tentatively let her fingers caress the strings and felt the notes vibrate through her entire body. Roberta's father walked through the main area where she sat with her eyes closed and stood for a few minutes watching and listening and then went in search of the harpist to find out where he could get her a harp.

The harp was delivered to the center one day while Roberta was at school, and she completely forgot that she and Judy were to go to the pool for a swim when she arrived home to find it sitting in the entryway. After that she would sit at the harp for hours each day when she got home from school and almost had to be forced to stop to do her homework or anything else. She felt as though she became one with the harp as her body resonated with each note. Where the flute sent her soaring through the air, the harp made her feel as though she were becoming one with the earth. She always saw colors swirling when she played and soon came to associate the different notes with colors.

Even though Roberta was preoccupied with her music, she and Judy remained close, and Judy was so grateful to her for the wonderful life she and Henry had now that she never resented the time Roberta spent with her music. She and Henry often talked privately about their parents and the life they had before, but they never discussed these things with anyone else.

Roberta came home from school one day very excited because there was going to be a dance at the school, and one of the boys had asked her to go with him. Aunt Helen and Lilith promised to help her get a dress, and that night she and Judy lay awake whispering until her father finally threatened to separate them if they didn't go to sleep. Judy also got asked to the dance later that week, so Helen and Lilith took both girls shopping that Saturday. Roberta got a beautiful pale pink dress with a very full skirt in three tiers that spread out around her when she turned, and Judy chose a simpler dress of deep blue that Lilith told her brought out the blue color of her eyes.

Two days before the dance the boy who had asked Roberta to go with him told her that his parents wouldn't let him go with her because her family was wicked and worshipped the devil. Roberta had no idea what he was talking about, but she felt as though someone had kicked her very hard and knocked all the breath out of her. She got through the rest of the day in a daze, and as soon as she got home she ran to find her father and began crying so hard he couldn't understand what she was saying. Judy told him what had happened, and for the first time since he had married Roberta's mother, Robert felt a strong desire to hurt someone.

The next day the girls did not go to school, and Robert went to talk to the principal and the teacher. When he told them what had happened, the teacher very haughtily remarked it was common knowledge that strange things went on at that place where the girls lived. Robert felt the urge to smash her face to wipe off that smug look, but this turned to compassion as he thought about how bitter her life must be. The principal seemed at a loss as to what to do, so Robert said that perhaps it would be best if the girls went to school elsewhere and left. He went immediately to talk to Lilith, who suggested the girls be sent to a school in town. The center had buses that went back and forth to town each day, so it would be no problem for them to drop the girls off and pick them up. Robert and Lilith drove into town that day and visited several of the schools until they found the one that they thought would be best for the girls. That night when the girls went to bed Judy started crying and told Roberta she was afraid of going to school in town. Roberta was also nervous, but she knew she had to be strong for Judy, so she assured Judy that she would take care of her and everything would be wonderful.

Chapter 3

The following morning Robert and Lilith took the girls to enroll in the new school, and when Roberta learned that the school offered music classes she forgot about being frightened and could hardly wait to get enrolled. The headmistress explained the classes to them and gave each girl a list of the things she would need. The girls were to start the next day, so they shopped for the necessary items before returning home. Their classes would not be exactly the same, and Roberta sensed that Judy was more frightened than ever. She talked to Lilith about this and Judy was told that if she ever needed anything she could call the center on the telephone that had recently been installed. Roberta awoke early the next morning eager to be on her way, but Judy had to be prodded to hurry. This school was completely different, and it seemed to Roberta that she rushed all day long just to get where she was supposed to be. On the ride home that evening Judy seemed worn out and very quiet, but Roberta talked excitedly about how much better this school was. At dinner that night she talked about how much nicer everyone was and how much better the classes were. Judy suddenly began to cry and told them that the teacher had said she would have to be put back a grade because she was not up to the level of the other students in her class. Judy had never done as well as Roberta, but everyone had assumed she would do well enough. Lilith promised to talk to the headmistress the following day and they all promised to help Judy study so that she would not have to go back a grade. After that every evening Roberta and Judy studied together with either Robert or Lilith to make sure that Judy really understood what she was studying. Within a month Judy had reached the level of the other students and finally began to enjoy school.

Roberta loved music class and was soon able to read music as well as the other students. She chose to play a traditional flute, which she quickly mastered and then asked to be allowed to play the harp. The only problem she had was in trying to play strictly by the music because she felt compelled to add her own interpretation. This became less of a problem once she could read the music fully, but the teacher still had to occasionally remind her not to improvise.

Roberta and Judy attended this school for the next eight years, and they both graduated with honors. Judy had been drawn to art and had become quite good at it while Roberta had mastered the flute, piccolo, xylophone, and harp. She had also learned to play the guitar on her own because this was not taught at the school. Both girls planned to attend college and had sent out many applications. They were both accepted by more than one college and so had a choice, but Judy was interested in working in advertising, and Roberta wanted to be a concert musician, so they would be going to different colleges. They vowed to spend most of their time together that summer realizing that this might be the last time they would have together like this, because their lives would be going in different directions.

Chapter 4

Shortly after the girls graduated Helen awoke one morning to find that Ted had passed away in his sleep. This was Roberta's first experience with death, and she became very moody and had trouble sleeping because she had dreams about all of the family dying and her being left all alone. The rest of the family talked about Uncle Ted as though he had just gone on a trip, and this made it even harder for Roberta to talk about her fears. One hot, sultry summer day when she and Judy had gone for a swim and were lying on the grass dosing, Judy noticed that Roberta had tears in her eyes and asked what was wrong. Roberta answered that she was afraid of everyone dying and leaving her alone. They talked about this, and after they returned to the house, Judy went to see Lilith and told her about Roberta's fears about death. Robert, Helen, Francis and Lilith tried to explain to Roberta that the body dies, but the real person merely changes and doesn't really leave at all. Roberta tried to believe what they told her, but she had never seen or heard her mother or anyone who had died, and she couldn't get over her fear of being left alone.

A few days later she went for a walk alone and suddenly found herself on a path leading to a beautiful little stone cottage that was surrounded by trees and flowers. This seemed very strange because she had walked here before and had never seen this cottage, but she felt a sort of peace settle over her as she walked up the path toward the door. Just as she reached to knock the door opened to reveal a strange little man who motioned her in and then disappeared without saying a word. Roberta stood in the doorway, and a deep sense of joy settled over her as she gazed around the small cottage. It seemed that each time she looked the room had changed.

LEGACY OF A MAGICAL COTTAGE

After a short while she noticed a table with a book on it and one chair in the middle of the room. She walked over to look at the book and suddenly remembered the story her father told about the magical stone cottage as she saw her name on the cover of the book. She opened the book and sat down to read. The story began with her birth, and tears spilled down her cheeks as she read about the death of her mother a week later. All the little details about her life were there, and she felt again the joys and sorrows she had experienced as though for the first time. She was not surprised when she reached the present to find that the remaining pages were blank. Movement caught her eye, and she looked up to see a woman and young girl standing in a shaft of light that streamed through an open window. The woman explained that she was her mother Anna and the young girl was her sister Diana. She said they were here to help her understand about life and death and the reason we are here on earth. As they talked, tears poured from Roberta's eyes, but she felt a love she had never known before. Anna told her how much she had loved her and how sad she had been to leave her, but that we each have a purpose in our life and hers had been finished. Anna told her that she was to do wonderful things with her music, and she should always follow her inner urging because this was her special gift and it could bring her everything she would want from life. They told her how they had always been with her, although she had been unaware of their presence, and that they would always be there when she needed them. After much too short a time, they said they had to leave and began to slowly fade away.

Roberta hurried home noticing that everything looked different, and she caught movement out of the corner of her eyes as she once again found herself in the open meadow and turned to find the cottage gone. She looked around and saw that there were little people all around and fairies flying through the air. She ran the rest of the way to the center and threw her arms around Robert's neck in excitement as she told him what had happened. Robert smiled as he saw Anna and Diana standing behind Roberta while she talked and said a silent prayer of thanks for their help. Roberta longed for more time with her mother and sister, but although they appeared frequently the rest of the summer, they faded away without speaking.

The girls were going to colleges out of state, and Lilith went along when Robert drove them both. Judy's college was the closest, so they stopped there first and helped her get settled before leaving the next day to drive Roberta to her college. Robert was relieved to see that Roberta no longer worried about death, and she was excited about embarking on the next phase of her life. As he gave her a final hug and kiss on the cheek, he felt a lump form in his chest for he knew that this was the last time he would see his little girl because she was becoming a young woman. He suddenly felt very lonely and dreaded returning to the house that he shared only with Hank since Francis was away at college. When they got back home, he suggested that Lilith and Helen share the house with him and Hank, and they could use the cabins for family visits and clients at the center. Both Helen and Lilith were happy to do this because they spent most of their time together, and the house seemed more like a home than the cabins, so their belongings were moved to the house the next day.

Chapter 5

The school that Roberta and Judy had attended was for girls only, and although Roberta had dated some, she had never been exposed to the kind of life that she encountered at college. She shared a room with another girl who never seemed to sleep or study, and there was always a party going on. She became caught up in the social life and found it difficult to keep up with her classes. Everyone drank alcohol, and she often found herself with a terrible hangover the day after a party, which made it difficult to concentrate in class. She dated several students but was not serious about any of them, and was just having a good time. After each test she promised herself that she would work harder, but then there would be another party and no time to study. When she got her grades at the end of the first semester, she was shocked to see how badly she had done and immediately made an appointment with a counselor to ask for help. She knew that her father was going to be very disappointed and hurt and made plans to move to another dormitory where there would be less temptation and she would be able to concentrate on schoolwork more.

The year passed quickly, and Roberta finally found a balance between her social life and studies, and her grades improved dramatically. She and Judy returned home for the summer vacation and spent most of their days lying by the pool talking about boys, clothes, makeup and all the things young girls talk about. Roberta enjoyed school and loved music, but she had not found any way that she could put it to use. She always kept her guitar and flute with her, and played while she and Judy talked during the summer.

Roberta returned to school in the fall and settled into a routine of classes, study, and social events. She had a new music teacher who had studied in Europe and taught them about the music of different cultures. Roberta fell in love with the music of Ireland and listened attentively when the teacher talked about the beautiful, lush green countryside and the people. The teacher noticed her interest and told her about a pub where Irish students went, and she went there with a friend one Friday night. There were people playing music, singing and dancing and she joined in and played the flute and even learned a couple of the dances and had a wonderful time. This quickly became her favorite place, and she would sit for hours listening to the Irish folklore and legends. She began to read everything that she could find about the Celts and the history of Ireland, and the more she read the more she longed to visit this wonderful place. She wrote to her father and told him that for Christmas that year she wanted a trip to Ireland during the summer vacation. Robert's first reaction was to refuse, but Lilith said she had always wanted to go to Ireland, and she would go with Roberta.

That night as Robert sat on the porch looking at the stars and listening to the sounds of the night Anna appeared and told him he should go also, so Robert wrote back and told Roberta that not only was she going to Ireland but he and Lilith were going with her. When her friends at the pub learned that she was going to Ireland that summer, they all made suggestions about where she should go and what she should see while she was there.

Francis and Judy were both home for Christmas, and Robert invited them to go to Ireland as well, but Francis was trying to finish medical school and didn't want to take the summer off. Judy surprised them by announcing that she couldn't go because she had fallen in love and was planning to be married as soon as they both finished school in two years.

Roberta returned to school, and dreamed of the coming trip. It seemed as though summer would never come, but the day finally arrived when she packed her things and piled everything in the car for the ride home. She was eager to get home to be with everyone and meet Judy's fiancé who was bringing her home that weekend.

They were to leave for Ireland in two weeks, and Roberta's friends had told her that Ireland is quite cool even in the summer, so she and Lilith spent hours shopping to find clothing that would be suitable. Robert teased them saying that if they didn't leave soon they wouldn't have enough money to make the trip.

The day finally came when they boarded the train that would take them to New York to the ship that would take them across the ocean to Ireland. They would be gone for more than a month, and Brian, Patrick, Laura and Doreen had been given full control over the center while they were gone. As the train sped across the landscape and night fell, Robert remembered the trip that he and Anna had taken to the ocean and wished that she was with them. As he fell asleep he saw Anna standing in the aisle and heard her whisper that she was looking forward to their trip because she had always wanted to go to Ireland.

Roberta had never been farther from home than college, and she discovered that she loved to travel. The constantly changing scenery and the knowledge that tomorrow they would reach New York made it impossible for her to sleep. After her father and Lilith fell asleep, she went to the observation car to keep from waking them. She watched as they raced past town after town and wondered about the people behind the curtains in the houses. She slept for brief periods and finally fell into an exhausted sleep just before dawn. The porter put a pillow under her head, covered her with a blanket and turned down the lantern before going to catch a short nap himself.

She awoke to the sound of the whistle announcing that they were approaching a crossing and sat up squinting her eyes against the glare of the early morning sun pouring through the windows. She suddenly realized that she was very hungry and went in search of her father and Lilith. They had just finished dressing when she got to their car, and the three of them hurried to the dining car before it became crowded. They ate breakfast and sipped coffee while Roberta read the notes she had made about the things they should do and see while in Ireland. Lilith and Roberta laughed as Robert groaned teasing her about having to stay the rest of their lives in order to do all that she had on her list. Late that afternoon they reached New York and were all very happy to be off the train. Since they would not be boarding the ship until the afternoon of the second day, they got rooms in a nice hotel where they washed off the dirt and grime of the trip before going to the dining room for dinner. They were all very tired and decided to get to bed early and get an early start sightseeing the next morning.

The noise and clamor of a city woke them early the next morning, and Robert and Lilith found themselves longing for the peaceful mornings in the country. Roberta, however, was fairly dancing with excitement and eager to get out into the hustle and bustle. They ate a hurried breakfast and then entered the throngs of people rushing about. Roberta had a map that showed all the highlights of the city, and by lunchtime Robert and Lilith were exhausted and ready to return to the hotel to rest until dinner. Robert insisted that Roberta not go out alone, and she returned to the lobby to pass the afternoon. The hotel manager saw how bored and restless she was and introduced her to his daughter Glena who offered to show Roberta the sights. Roberta raced up the stairs and burst into Robert's room causing him to drop the book he was reading and leap to his feet in alarm. She apologized for startling him and begged to be allowed to go sightseeing with Glena. Robert accompanied Roberta to the lobby to meet the girl and verify that she was, indeed, the manager's daughter and then kissed Roberta on the cheek and told them to be back before dark. He returned to his room feeling a little guilty because of his relief at having someone else take over as chaperone for his very energetic daughter. However, that evening as it grew later and darkness approached, Robert began to pace the lobby and fret reproaching himself for being negligent and imagining all the horrible disasters that could have befallen Roberta. It was with great relief that he saw the two girls enter the lobby just as the streetlights came on. The girls said goodbye and Robert thanked Glena for showing Roberta the sights while Roberta ran to the room she was sharing with Lilith to freshen up and change for dinner.

Roberta was very tired and was happy to return to their room after dinner. While they ate, they talked about the city, and she told them about all the wonderful things she had seen with Glena that she would have missed because they were not on the map. They all agreed that it is probably best to have someone who lives in a place show you around rather than relying on information provided for tourists. They were to board the ship the next afternoon and made plans to do some light sightseeing in the morning and then rest after lunch until time to go to the dock for boarding.

As they walked through the streets the following morning Lilith noticed an art gallery that she had dealt with before she retired and suggested they go in. Lilith asked to speak to the manager and while they talked, Robert and Roberta wandered around looking at the paintings. Robert stopped suddenly as he recognized the special glade with the waterfall where he and Anna had made love many years before. The painting was of the waterfall with the faint outline of a woman's figure in the falling water and elementals at work and play throughout the glade. He had never seen this particular painting, and it brought back many memories. Roberta came over and immediately knew that this was one of her mother's paintings. They stood in silence for a long time, and then Robert told her about the day that Anna had taken him there and begged him to let her help him support his family and then left when he refused without telling him about the child she carried. He went on to tell her how he later learned about Francis and found Lilith who finally agreed to take him to Anna. Roberta had never heard anything about this and had assumed that her mother and father had just fallen in love and gotten married. She suddenly realized that she really didn't know the people who were her parents and asked her father if he would tell her more about her mother and their lives. Robert gave her a hug and whispered he would love to as Lilith and the manager joined them. Lilith explained to the manager that this was the husband and daughter of the woman who had painted the picture they were looking at. He turned to Roberta and asked if she also painted and seemed quite disappointed to learn that she didn't share her mother's talent. He explained that he had many requests for Anna's work and could have sold the painting they were looking at many times but it was the last one he had, and he couldn't bring himself to part with it.

Chapter 6

They boarded the ship that afternoon, and while the ship crossed the ocean Robert kept his promise to tell Roberta about his life and her mother's as they sat in deck chairs and watched the constantly moving ocean. Lilith often joined them and added details about Anna that Robert didn't know, and Roberta felt as though she had met both of her parents for the first time. She saw the deep love in Robert's eyes as he talked about Anna and the pain and loneliness when he talked about his family. She had only seen her father's family a few times but understood why he felt the way he did when he talked about them.

Four days out they ran into a storm, and most of the passengers stayed in their cabins too seasick to leave their bunks. Robert had brought along some medication for this and none of them suffered from seasickness. Roberta was fascinated by the violence of the storm and stayed on deck until Robert insisted she to go indoors to avoid being washed overboard. The storm had begun to abate by dinner; however, eating was quite an adventure as they struggled to catch their plates and keep everything from sliding off the table. Roberta finally gave up and made a sandwich and sat back to enjoy the show, and Robert and Lilith followed her example. Roberta laughed until she had tears in her eyes as she watched those at other tables struggle to maintain their table manners and decorum, and Robert and Lilith scolded her as they fought back their own smiles.

The storm had blown itself out by the next day, and the remainder of the crossing was uneventful. They were all looking forward to getting off the ship and as they had been told that they would reach land by early morning Roberta insisted on sleeping in a deck chair so that she would not miss the first sight of Ireland. Robert couldn't allow her to sleep on deck alone, and he grumbled as he gathered a blanket and pillow to join her. He fell asleep thinking that she should have been a little more like her mother only to hear Anna whisper that she was very much like her mother and smiled as he realized how true this was.

Robert awoke to the sound of the ship's whistle to find Roberta standing at the railing mesmerized as the deep green shores of Ireland came ever closer. He went to stand beside her and was grateful to his headstrong daughter for his being on deck to see this beautiful sight.

As Roberta stood at the rail, she felt something tugging deep inside and a strange, overwhelming feeling of homecoming. It was afternoon before the ship finally docked, and she had never left the deck except when absolutely necessary all morning. Robert and Lilith even brought her food because she wouldn't stay inside long enough to eat. It was as though she was under some spell, and they began to wonder if this trip might have been a mistake after all.

One of Roberta's friends from the pub had given her the name of a hotel, and they were soon settled in rooms that were very quaint but comfortable. Robert and Lilith wanted to just get something to eat and relax, but Roberta couldn't wait to go exploring. Robert inquired about tours and arranged for Roberta to join one that afternoon and evening while he and Lilith planned a more quiet tour of the town with an early dinner and relaxing at the hotel. By evening only the younger people remained with the tour, and Roberta had a wonderful time as they visited different pubs. She was very comfortable with the local people and told them about her friends at college. She had taken her flute with her and joined the local people playing and singing. It was well after midnight by the time she returned to the hotel, but she was not tired and decided to sit in the lobby for a while before going to the room she shared with Lilith. Because it was so late, there were few guests around, and she talked to those who worked at the hotel. She told them that she wanted to get away from the places that tourists go and stay in a small village. One of the girls who worked in the kitchen was from a small village about 40 kilometers inland, and she told Roberta how to get a bus to take her there and who to see to get a couple of rooms.

Robert and Lilith had expected to spend a couple of days in town and were surprised the next morning when Roberta announced she wanted to leave that day.

They were even more surprised when she told them about the small town, the place they could stay and how they could get there. It seemed that Roberta had things under control and all they had to do was sit back and enjoy the trip. They packed and made arrangements for the trip that afternoon before having a leisurely breakfast and doing some last minute shopping. They all needed sturdier shoes than they had been able to buy at home and some rain gear, which they purchased before leaving.

As they rode across the rugged, lush countryside, they all became very quiet. For the first time since Roberta had stumbled on the stone cottage, she saw elementals everywhere and felt the magic that she had felt that day. Robert also saw the elementals and felt a sense of magic in the air while Lilith only sensed the things they were seeing and envied their special gift. When they reached the village it was as though they had stepped back in time. The house was very simple and rustic, and while Lilith would have preferred a few more modern amenities Roberta instantly fell under the spell of this wonderful place. That evening after dinner, they all went to the local pub to pass the time and become acquainted with the people. Roberta took her flute and after listening to the local musicians play for a while asked if she could join in. She was still playing and dancing when Robert and Lilith were ready to leave and the pub owner told them he would see she got home safely. An older man came in shortly after they left with a small musical instrument that sounded like a harp but lay across his legs, and Roberta was fascinated by it. She asked about the instrument and was told that it was a lap harp. She told him that she played a regular harp and asked if she could try the lap harp. He happily gave her the instrument and pointed out some of the differences as she began to tentatively caress the strings. She had always wished that there were some way to take her harp with her the way she did her flute, and she could barely wait until the next morning to talk to her father about getting a lap harp.

Roberta awoke while it was still dark the following morning and hurriedly dressed in warm clothing and the rugged shoes she had bought the day before. She walked until she came to a stream that tumbled over and around rocks that had been polished smooth by the waters of many years and sat down on a large rock to play her flute. She closed her eyes and matched the rhythm of the stream and the call of the wildlife as she saw the colors of the rainbow blending and whirling around her. She had no idea how much time had passed, but when she opened her eyes and looked around it was fully daylight, and she could hear the sounds of people in the village. There were many elementals going about their day working and playing among the undergrowth. As she sat reveling in the beauty of the scene, Roberta felt the desire to try painting in order to share this with others.

She ran back to the house very excited to talk to her father about the lap harp and also some basic painting supplies. She told them about the harp first and then hesitantly said that she wanted to try painting. Robert and Lilith were both very surprised about the painting, as she had shown no interest in anything other than music before. She talked about the strong feeling she had of wanting to preserve and share the beauty of this country with others, and as she talked Robert saw Anna appear behind her and smile before fading away. After breakfast, the three of them went for a walk, and Robert agreed that the beauty was very compelling. They found a shop in the small village that sold limited painting supplies and purchased what they had, but they were told they would have to go to a larger town to find a lap harp.

Once again, Roberta was up early the next morning and left after eating a hasty breakfast. She found a secluded spot overlooking the stream to practice her painting and worked diligently trying to manipulate the colors to capture what she saw. After several hours she was becoming quite frustrated when she looked up to see her mother standing beside her. Anna told her take a deep breath and picture the colors that she wanted as she began to mix the paints. Roberta felt as though she were in a trance as her mother whispered to her while she mixed the colors. Finally the colors were mixed, and she began to paint. She seemed to feel a light touch on her hand as though it was being guided as she painted the stream and rugged landscape with elementals working around the flowers and fairies flying overhead. She was unaware of anything except this world and jumped as though awakened from sleep when she heard Robert call her name. He said they had become worried about her when she didn't come back for lunch and it began to get dark. He helped her gather her paints as Roberta held up the painting and told him about her mother helping her. Though the painting was quite rough, he had no doubt that Anna had guided their daughter's hand and that with her mother's help she could be very good.

The area around the small village was rich in ancient Celtic and medieval ruins, and they rented a horse and lorry to visit these sites. Robert and Lilith wandered among the ruins enjoying the energies and talking about the rich history of the area as Roberta played the flute or painted as her mood dictated. One day when they visited one of the stone monuments, Roberta painted the huge stones, as they must have originally appeared with people in hooded capes participating in some religious ceremony. Robert approached her while she was working and withdrew a short distance as he saw that she appeared to be in an almost trance state. He later discussed this with Lilith who told him that Anna had often appeared that way when she painted and seemed to actually become a part of the scene she was painting.

After four days Lilith announced she couldn't stand another day of coarse sheets, no heat and no hot water. They agreed to visit another larger city on the southeastern coast before making their way back north to board the ship the following week. The bus would not be leaving until noon, so

Roberta dressed hurriedly and left while the others were still asleep for one last walk through the countryside that seemed to pull at the very core of her being. She sat beside the stream, which seemed to whisper to her of secrets to be learned if she were to stay, and she knew that she would be returning to this enchanted land. Robert was just putting on his coat to go find her when he saw her turn to take one last look before returning to the house to pack.

They reached the town just before dinner, and Roberta teased Lilith that she thought she was going to kiss the hotel clerk when he told them that the rooms were heated and hot water was available whenever they wanted a bath. The food they had eaten in the village had been plain and substantial, and they all enjoyed the more enticing fare offered at the hotel. Roberta had gotten up very early that morning and even she was happy to go to bed early that night. As she snuggled into the soft, smooth sheets, she had to admit that they certainly felt better than what they had been sleeping on. That night she dreamed about looking down on a beautiful, green island as she floated on a cloud high above the trees.

The following morning found Roberta energized and eager to be on the move. Lilith absolutely refused to leave the luxury of the hotel before dinner, so Robert and Roberta set out on the quest to find her a simple lap harp. They found several stores that sold the smaller version of a regular harp, but Roberta insisted she wanted the simpler one that rested on the lap or a table. Just as they were about to give up, they passed a small shop with windows full of various items and Roberta suggested they go in and have a look around. The shop was fascinating with barely enough room to walk between the tables and shelves that were piled high with everything imaginable. They found some very unique, inexpensive gifts for the family and friends at home and were making their way back to the front of the store when Roberta saw a harp like the one she wanted on a high shelf. Robert supported her as she stepped on the lower shelves to reach it, and they both began to cough as dust that had been undisturbed for years covered them. The harp seemed to be in good shape, and the man even gave her some extra strings for it. They left the shop with their purchases very happy to get back out in the fresh air where they could breathe and brush off some of the dust. When they reached the hotel, Lilith asked if they had crawled all over the town to get so dirty and dusty and said she was glad she hadn't been with them when they described the shop. They cleaned up and changed their clothes and then met in the lobby to discuss plans for the rest of their visit.

They stayed one day enjoying the sites and then caught a bus early the next morning to start north to board the ship for home. As they rode through the countryside stopping at each small town, Roberta painted the scenery and felt as though she was saying goodbye to a dear friend she had recently rediscovered. They stayed overnight at several towns along the way, and each time went to a local pub where she played her flute and the lap harp. Robert and Lilith marveled at how she fit in and seemed to be so at home wherever they went. They reached the town where they were to board the ship the day before it was to sail and spent the time doing some last minute shopping for gifts to take home.

Chapter 7

When they boarded the ship the following morning, Roberta stood at the rail watching as the beautiful, mysterious Ireland slowly disappeared from view. On the voyage home, she painted feverishly as though trying to capture the essence of the country she had just left before the memory faded. Robert and Lilith stayed close by but never intruded on her when she was painting. She took the harp on deck and played in the evening, and the captain invited her to play in the salon for the other passengers. She thanked him for the offer but said she preferred to play outside on the deck.

The ship docked very early in the morning, so they decided to catch the train at once to get back home. As Roberta sat looking out the train's windows she noted that the colors of the landscape seemed dull and subdued compared to the deep, rich green of Ireland, and she felt strangely homesick. They arrived in town in time to catch the last bus as it returned to the center and surprised everyone as they were sitting down to eat. There was much merriment that night as they talked about the trip and all the strange and wonderful things they had seen. No one mentioned Roberta's paintings, but she did show them the new instrument she had discovered and played for them after dinner. It was very late when they walked the trail on the way to the little house that Anna had bought when she first moved here. Roberta had felt her mother's presence very much on the trip and she was not surprised to see her standing in the road ahead with her grandmother, grandfather and Diana as though welcoming them home. This was the second time that Helen had seen her sister since her death, and tears of joy filled her eyes. Lilith was the only one who was unable to see this and once again, she was filled with envy of their wonderful gift.

Roberta returned to school eager to tell her friends about the trip to Ireland and settled once again into a routine of school and social events. Most of her evenings were spent in the pub with her Irish friends where she played the flute, lap harp, or guitar and sometimes sang. She had taken the pictures of Ireland to school with her, and several times she took them out late at night and fell asleep thinking about Ireland and dreaming of being back there.

Christmas was a very big, glorious affair at the center, as usual, with singing, dancing and food of every description imaginable, and Roberta enjoyed being back with her family and friends. She noticed that Lilith seemed very frail and talked to her father who told her that he was concerned. He said they had been doing healings, but she didn't seem to be getting better. Two days after Christmas, Lilith told them that her mother Lynette and Anna had appeared to her the night before and told her that it was time for her to join them. She was thrilled that she had finally seen what they all saw and happy to be joining her mother and Anna. She had talked to her attorney the week before and made arrangements for her funeral. Francis and Judy had both planned to leave that day but cancelled their plans to stay with the family. They all spent the day reminiscing about the past while Roberta played music and they sang when she played songs that they knew. Lilith gave Robert the name and address of the gallery where they had gone while in New York and told him that if Roberta decided to paint he would be glad sell her paintings for her. As the sun dipped below the horizon that evening, Lilith took one final deep breath and passed gently away. Robert, Roberta and Francis sat watching as a hazy form lifted from the body and went to join the shining forms of Lynette and Anna who were waiting. Lilith had been more family than many of the family members and all of them took her loss hard, but it was especially hard for Helen as she was the only one remaining of her age group. The service was held at the center and it was crammed with people who had known Lilith when she had her gallery. Her body was placed in the small plot that had been designated as a cemetery for family members when Anna had passed. After the funeral, Lilith's attorney told Robert that he was Lilith's sole heir, and they were all shocked to learn that Lilith had left a very large fortune in money and property. She had also left a note telling him that most of that money had been made from the sale of Anna's paintings and rightly belonged to her family.

All of the children were in college now, and Helen and Robert would be alone in the house after the holidays. Roberta was the last of the children to leave, and she got a lump in her throat because they looked so lonely as she drove away, but she saw her mother and Lilith standing beside them and knew that they would be watched over. They had talked about Patrick and Laura possibly moving into the cabin next to the house because the center had continued to grow and their cabin could be used for clients who needed to stay for long-term treatment.

Chapter 8

Roberta once again settled into her college routine but called often to talk to Robert and Helen and wished she could be there with them. Shortly before the end of the year she realized that she was bored with college and dreaded the thought of another year of wasted time. She still spent most of her evenings at the pub, which was the only thing time that she was not very lonely and homesick.

A stranger began coming in night after night but just sat at a corner table and never talked to anyone or joined in. This made them all a little nervous, and the men made certain that one or two of them accompanied her and the other women when they left as a precaution. The man had been coming to the pub almost every night for a couple of weeks when he approached her one night, handed her a business card and said he would like to talk to her. Roberta almost fainted when he explained that he was from a record company and would like to record some of her music. They talked for a while about how everything would be handled, and he gave her what he said was a standard contract. Roberta knew nothing about this business, and she told him she would have to talk to her father before she signed anything. Lilith appeared that night as she drifted off to sleep and told her to have her attorney look over the contract before she signed it. Roberta only had one class on Friday, so she decided to skip it and drive home for the weekend to talk to her father.

Robert called Lilith's attorney who came out Saturday to look over the contract and told them his only concern was the length of time. They made arrangements for him to negotiate on her behalf and spent the rest of the time visiting and catching up on the news before she left to drive back to college the following day. A week later Roberta received a letter from the attorney with a contract for her to sign and give to Mr. Hanson, from the record company, who was to contact her in a few days. She was very excited about the idea of recording her music but felt lonely and wished she could talk about this with everyone over dinner at the center. Mr. Hanson came into the pub a couple of days later to get the contract and told her he had arranged for the recording studio on Saturday.

She arrived at the studio early with her lap harp, flute and guitar and gave the lady behind the desk her name. She had barely gotten settled on a sofa to wait when Mr. Hanson came over, picked up her guitar case, and led her through a door behind the desk. He had made notes on the songs that he would like for her to play and sing, and they discussed these as she settled herself on the stool behind the microphone. Roberta began to play, but the music sounded very strained because of her nervousness. After several attempts without success, Mr. Hanson told the men in the recording booth to just begin recording whenever they thought it was right without telling Roberta. He went into the booth with her and told her to just start playing while they talked in order to get used to being there. After about 10 minutes Roberta had relaxed and was playing the way she did in the pub. He stayed in the booth with her, talking between songs and only told her that she had been recorded when she voiced concern about wasting so much time. By then she was completely relaxed, so the session was finished without any further problem.

The contract called for her to record a record every couple of months for a total of five records. The record company had the final say on which songs were recorded; however, most of the time they listened when she made suggestions. She was at the recording studio every weekend and by summer break she had recorded two records. She had arranged to return to record for one week each month during the summer break, and one of her friends from the pub invited Roberta to stay with her when she was in town.

Roberta had three final exams on Monday and one on Tuesday morning, so she went to the pub Monday night to say goodbye to everyone. She was up early Tuesday morning and packed everything in the car so that she could leave as soon as she finished her last exam. The drive seemed to take forever, and during the drive home, she had to really watch her speed because in her eagerness to get there she caught herself driving much too fast several times.

She arrived during her favorite part of the day when everyone was at the center eating dinner and visiting before going their separate ways for the night. She stopped in the doorway to absorb the scene and her eyes misted over with love for these wonderful people. Robert had his back to her, and she motioned for everyone to be quiet as she sneaked up from behind and gave him a big hug. They made room for her to sit beside her father and Doreen brought her a plate. Roberta had missed all of the good, fresh food they had at the center and ate until she was afraid she would be sick. As she ate, she told them about the recording sessions and the plans for recording over the summer and got caught up on their news of things at home. She walked home in the moonlight with her father and Aunt Helen, and then sat in the swing on the porch long after they had gone to bed letting the harmony and magic of home restore her spirit. It was a little lonely because Judy had gotten married before finishing college, and Henry spent most of his time with her and her husband Tom. She missed her friend but knew that the time had come for them to go their separate ways.

During the summer when she was home between recording sessions she helped out with the canning and preserving at the center in the morning, played the harp and flute at the center on Saturdays and spent the hot afternoons beside the pool alone or with the others playing her flute, guitar or lap harp. One lazy afternoon during the hottest part of the summer when she was alone dosing beside the pool in the secluded grove, Anna appeared and told her she should compose her own music from her heart rather than playing music others had written. She sat up still half asleep and reached for her flute and began to play with her eyes closed. She had some paper with her that she had brought to write a letter to her friends, so she made notes as she got a section the way that she wanted it. She had not seen colors when she played for a long time, but now she saw the colors whirl and blend as the notes filled the air with sounds that brought visions of angels and fairies.

She was startled when she opened her eyes to see a strange little man very much like the one who had welcomed her at the stone cottage sitting beside her. They sat in silence for a while until he suddenly remarked that she had a talent every bit as great as her mother's and should find a way to share it with the world. She asked if he had known her mother, and he said he had helped her to develop her art and had been there whenever she needed a friend, and he would be there for Roberta too whenever she needed him. Each day she returned to the pool or sought out another secluded place and worked writing her own music, and the gnome often joined her. In the evenings, she would sit on the porch in the moonlight and play the harp and write words or put the finishing touches on the pieces she had written. She had told her father and Aunt Helen about her mother and the gnome coming to her about the music, and they encouraged her to spend as much time as possible with her music.

Chapter 9

She made two records during the summer and tried to get them to let her play some of her own music, but they had insisted on music that everyone was familiar with and were unwilling to take a chance. She was glad she only had to do one more record to fulfill her contract so that she could concentrate on her own music and hopefully find someone who would record it.

The closer it came to time to return for her last year in college, the more Roberta knew that she just could not go back. Aunt Helen was very frail now, and she did not want to miss the time with her for something that seemed so useless and empty. She dreaded talking to her father about dropping out of college and waited until a day when she felt the time was right before broaching the subject with him. To her dismay, he smiled and said her mother had prepared him for this, and she should make her own decision.

She contacted Mr. Hanson to let him know that she was not returning to college and would be free to stay in town for a full week to make the next record. The records that they had made were doing fairly well, and she was receiving money from their sale, but this was not what she was interested in. By the time of the next recording session, she had finished two instrumentals and two songs of her own, and she took the music for these with her. She asked to meet Mr. Hanson before the session to play these for him and asked that they be included on this record, but he said this just wasn't the kind of music he wanted to record. It took just over a week to finish the final record, and on the last day Mr. Hanson brought her a new contract to sign. He was obviously taken by surprise when

Roberta thanked him for the opportunity he had given her but refused to sign explaining that she wanted to do her own music. Mr. Hanson tried to change her mind, offering a larger percentage and even offering to include one of her original pieces on each new record, but she remained firm in her decision.

She went to the pub every night before she returned home and stayed late because she knew it might be a long while before she saw her friends again. They laughed, played music, sang and talked about Ireland and their plans for the future. When she left that last night, she said goodbye with tears in her eyes and invited them to visit her any time. Jaime, one of the young men that she had been closest to, walked with her to the hotel where she was staying and asked if he could visit her when he took his vacation in a few weeks. She told him she would enjoy that very much and wrote out directions with the phone number of the center in case he should get lost. The drive home was uneventful, and she enjoyed the feeling of being free from college and able to do whatever she wanted with her music.

Once home, she helped out at the center, practiced the harp there for a few hours every day and played all day on Saturdays. She had contacted everyone she could think of about recording her music without success and began to wonder if she had been too hasty refusing to sign with Mr. Hanson again. However, she remembered what her mother had told her about following her inner feelings with regard to her music and knew that it would work out for the best even if it did take a while.

Although she was glad to be away from college, she missed all of her friends from the pub and was very happy to see Jaime a couple of weeks later. He arrived on a hot afternoon, and after introducing him to her father and Aunt Helen she suggested they go for a swim to cool off. After they had changed, she led him to the pool where they played in the nice cool water for a while and then stretched out on the grass to talk. Jaime had brought his flute and that evening after dinner he joined her as she played the harp and her flute. The next afternoon they took the musical instruments and the music she had written to the pool when they went for a swim. She had started a new piece, and the two of them worked on it for hours playing the piece over and over and making changes until they were satisfied with each part before moving on to the next. They laughed and talked as they worked, and Roberta realized she had missed Jaime more than she realized. Robert and Helen came for a swim to cool off and stayed for a while listening as they dried off. As he walked back to the house, Robert wondered if Roberta was aware of Jaime's love for her. She had told him that Jaime was just one of her friends from the pub, but he could see that there was more to it than that for Jaime.

The piece of music was finished the following day, and Roberta knew it was better than any she had done alone. They decided to go for a swim, and as she rose to her feet, Jaime offered his hand to help her up and then pulled her into his arms and kissed her lingeringly on the lips. Her lips parted under the gentle prodding of his tongue, which sent shivers of ecstasy throughout her body. Their bathing suits left a lot of skin exposed and Roberta felt fire building throughout her body as she became acutely aware of the feel of his body pressed against hers. She stood dazed as he moved back slightly in order to look into her eyes, and as she looked into his eyes, she felt a stirring within the very core of her being. They stood for a long time without moving, and then he kissed her quickly on the lips and turned away.

They silently moved to the pool and slipped into the water where they swam for a while before returning to sit side by side on the grassy bank. Jaime said he had known how he felt for a long time but had not said anything because her family obviously had money, and he really had nothing to offer her. Then, when she had come to the pub that last night and told them she wouldn't be coming back to make more records, he knew he had to see her again and had asked if he could visit even though the thought of coming here scared him to death. She said she had always considered him just a friend but admitted that during the time he had been here, her feelings seemed to be deepening. They talked about how much they had enjoyed working together on the music and how wonderful it would be if they could work together all of the time.

They continued to work on the music each day and occasionally went into town and of course they played and sang their music in the evening after dinner. When he left at the end of the week, Roberta felt as though a part of her was missing but was not sure if she truly loved Jaime or just the idea of being in love. They talked on the telephone frequently and wrote often, and each time she heard his voice her heart began to beat faster. At her father's suggestion, she invited Jaime to join them for Christmas, and, although he was expected to spend the holiday with his family, he accepted. He arranged to take more time off from work so he would arrive late on Christmas Eve and stay until New Year's Day.

On Christmas Eve she helped with the final preparations and then hurried back to the house to clean up and dress before Jaime arrived. She had just started back to the center when she saw his car coming up the lane to the house. As she approached the car, he got out and moved to take her in his arms. When his arms closed around her and his lips claimed hers, Roberta's doubts about her love for him vanished in the storm of emotions that washed over her. She felt as though she had come home and was complete in a way she had never been before. Instead of returning to the center, he drove to the house where they sat on the porch in the gathering darkness and talked.

Robert had sent Jaime to the house so that they could have some time alone, and when they didn't return he asked Laura to fix two plates of food to take to them. When he and Helen approached the house in the car, because Helen could no longer walk the distance to and from the center, he saw Roberta and Jaime sitting in the swing and suddenly felt very lonely as he remembered the times that he and Anna had sat like that looking at the stars and talking far into the night. Robert helped Helen up the steps and when he handed Roberta the food he had brought for them, she suddenly realized she was very hungry and quite cold. Helen and Robert went to bed while Roberta and Jaime sat at the table eating and talking in whispers. All of the cabins and rooms at the center were full because of the holiday, so Jaime and Francis were to share Roberta's room while Roberta would share Helen's room. After one last kiss, they reluctantly went to their rooms long after midnight.

The center rang with laughter Christmas Day as everyone enjoyed a wonderful day with a large meal and gifts being exchanged, but the reason for the celebration was emphasized with songs and prayer, and Jaime said he had never been so aware of the meaning of Christmas. They all helped clean up after the celebration and then went home loaded with food and gifts.

Francis was home and had finished all of his medical training. He wanted to work at the center, but he and Robert agreed that he should have a practice in town as well because the center was so isolated. They planned to go into town to look for space on Monday after Christmas. The attorney had notified Robert that he needed to check on a house that Lilith had owned, so they planned to combine this with finding space for Francis to establish his practice. Robert had not realized that the house was the one where Lilith had lived, and both of them were flooded with memories when he pulled up to the address he had been given by the attorney. Lilith had rented the house to a friend rather than sell it, and the woman, who was very old, had recently died. Everything was in disrepair, the beautiful courtyard was overgrown with weeds, and the pool that Francis had loved so much as a boy was full of dirt and debris. Robert could see no reason to keep the house and said they should stop by the attorney's office on the way home to have him handle selling it, but Francis asked him to keep it since he would need a place to live in town if he was to have a practice here. Robert pointed out how much work would have to be done to make the place livable again, but Francis said he had loved this house and wanted to live here. Robert finally agreed and said they could have the men from the center do a lot of the work since there wasn't much going on there this time of year, and they planned to get started on the repairs right away.

On New Year's day Roberta awoke early, dressed quietly and left the room to avoid waking Helen. Jaime was to leave that day, and she didn't want to waste a minute of the time they had left sleeping. When it was almost time to go to the center for breakfast, Roberta went to wake Helen and discovered she was not breathing. Francis checked her and said that she had passed away sometime during the night and calls were placed to the sheriff and to Helen's oldest daughter. Roberta was very glad she had not gone back to college and had been here to share her great aunt's last days.

Jaime was surprised at the reaction of Roberta's family to Helen's death, and Roberta took him aside to explain their beliefs about life and death. Jaime had noticed that Robert talked about his wife as though she was alive at times, but he had thought this was just because he missed her. As Roberta talked to him about her family's ability to see things others couldn't and actually talk to those who had passed from this life, he looked at her as though she had suddenly gone crazy. He had been raised in a strict Protestant home, and the things that she talked about were what the church warned were associated with the devil. A lot of things had puzzled him about the center and what went on there, but he had been so preoccupied with Roberta that he had pushed these things away. He kissed her goodbye that day very stiffly, and Roberta's heart sank as she watched him drive away without looking back.

She bundled up against the cold and went to sit by the pool to think about everything that had happened. She knew that if Jaime's love was real he would be back and if not it was better to know now, but a couple of tears made their way down her cheeks as she thought about never seeing him again. She suddenly became aware that she wasn't alone and turned to see the gnome sitting beside her. He talked to her about how we learn from relationships and this helps us to have understanding for others.

Chapter 10

The Saturday after Jaime left she played the music that she and Jaime had written for the flute at the center as well as some pieces she had written for the harp and flute. She noticed one of the clients who had been at the center during the holidays undergoing treatment sitting where he could listen to her play and sing. When she took a break in the afternoon, he approached and asked where she got her music. Roberta told her that she wrote it herself and a friend had helped her with the one piece. He told her that he owned several restaurants in New York City and would like to buy her music for his entertainers to play. He made her a very generous offer, and she agreed to sell a couple of the pieces but refused to sell the one that she and Jaime had written.

By spring Francis had his office open in town, and Lilith's house was back to a habitable state. Roberta spent a lot of time helping with painting and cleaning to take her mind off missing Jaime, and she and Francis became very close. They were working together one evening with the radio on when she stopped working to listen to a song that was on the radio. It seemed somehow familiar, and she suddenly realized that it was one of the pieces of music she had sold, but it had been changed and was now loud and irritating instead of soft and soothing. She swore that day to never sell a piece of music again without having control over what happened to it and said a prayer of thanksgiving that she had not sold the piece she and Jaime had written.

The center had grown far beyond what it was when Robert and Anna first started it and had become a very successful business. Patrick and Brian had been given shares in the business and had full control of the day-to-day operation, so Robert became less and less involved. He and Roberta stayed more and more at Lilith's old house in town while they worked on it. As he worked cleaning up the courtyard and restoring it, he realized how much he missed working with the earth and a simpler life. He began going to the church and the restaurant where their friends used to go and enjoyed reminiscing with the few people who remembered Lilith and Anna. Each Friday evening Robert, Francis and Roberta stayed at the house in the country and Francis worked at the center while Roberta played and sang on Saturday; but Robert felt as though he didn't belong there and soon began just staying at the house where he felt closer to Anna.

One Sunday at church a woman, who had been a close friend of Lilith, introduced Robert to her daughter Edna. Edna's husband had died a few months earlier, and she had moved back home to take care of her mother who was too ill to live alone. She had known Anna and Lilith, and the three of them went with several others to the restaurant for lunch where Robert and Edna talked about Anna, Lilith, her husband and their children. He was surprised when she said that she felt she didn't belong anywhere anymore and told her he had been feeling the same way. After that he and Edna saw each other several times a week, and when her mother died a few months later, he and Edna announced that they were going to be married and would live in her mother's home. They each put everything except a modest amount into trust funds for their children so there wouldn't be any grumbling about anyone losing their inheritance.

Roberta had sensed Robert's loneliness and was happy that he had someone to share his life with. They had all lived in Lilith's house and she still shared the house with Francis, but he worked late and had a busy social life, so after Robert moved she found herself alone a lot. One evening when she couldn't stand spending another night alone, she looked in the phone book and found a bar that advertised it was like an Irish pub. When she arrived, she found the bar was filled with a very rough, very drunk crowd and left without even sitting down. She hated to go back to the empty house and just drove aimlessly through the streets. She was thinking about driving out to the center for a visit when she noticed a small bar in a poor but quiet part of town. She parked her car and entered the bar to find a few people tossing darts while others played primarily Irish music and sang. Roberta got a beer and went to sit at a secluded table to listen to the music. She sipped her beer slowly and then left.

The following evening Roberta returned to the bar with her flute and lap harp and asked if they would mind her joining them. An older man commented on her lap harp saying he hadn't seen one of those since leaving Ireland, and she told him she had gotten it on a trip to Ireland. She enjoyed the evening very much and soon developed the habit of going there three or four times a week to play, sing and talk about Ireland.

Since Robert, Francis, and Roberta were all living in town now, Patrick and Brian approached Robert about buying the house where they had lived as the center needed more room to grow, and after talking it over with Francis and Roberta, he agreed to sell. The center was becoming more and more businesslike, and Roberta felt that her playing was not really appreciated anymore. It was with mixed emotions that they packed the few belongs still there, including her harp, into a truck for the move to town. The three of them went one last time to the pool, and as they sat talking about the many happy days they had spent here Anna, Diana, Lilith, Helen and Ted appeared on the other side of the pool and smiled and waved before slowly fading away. They walked slowly back to the truck commenting on the orchard, the bridge across the stream, the swings on the porches and all the other things that had made this home special. As they climbed into the truck, they heard loud music and laughter coming from the direction of the center and knew that the time had indeed come to move on.

Chapter 11

Roberta dated some but spent most of her time practicing and writing music and began to paint a little now and then. She often saw her mother and Lilith in the courtyard of the house and felt very much at home there. She began to feel as though she should do something with her music and was relieved when Mr. Hanson called shortly after they moved to town and said he would like to talk to her about recording some of her music. He agreed to come to her since it would be easier than for her to try to bring everything to him, and she would be able to play all of her instruments. Roberta asked Troy and Branden, two of the men she played with regularly at the bar to accompany her, and after hearing them play Mr. Hanson agreed they were very good together. It took three days for them to agree on 12 songs to be recorded. Roberta signed a contract for only three records with the stipulation that she would have final say on the choice of music and her accompaniment.

She told Mr. Hanson that she would let him know when they were ready. The three of them practiced for a month before she felt they were ready to record and Troy and Branden could arrange to be gone for a week. They traveled to the recording studio in her car, and she paid them a generous amount for each day they were gone and paid for a room for them. The actual recording only took four days, and everyone was happy with the result at the end of that time. She would have liked to go to the pub to see her old friends while in town but felt this would not be wise given the situation between her and Jaime.

Roberta arrived back home to find the house in a mess as Francis packed and unpacked in preparation for moving. He had been offered the opportunity to work in a teaching hospital in Chicago with the latest equipment and research facilities. He said he hoped to be able to teach the young doctors that being a good doctor requires more than just treating the physical body. The center had become more a spa than a healing center, and shortly after they sold the house there Francis had stopped going, so there was nothing holding him here. He made arrangements to have another doctor take over his practice and left two weeks later. She waved goodbye as he drove away and then returned to the house where she stood in the middle of the living room feeling very alone and vulnerable. She went to sit beside the pool and began to cry. A figure that seemed to be all light appeared in the corner of the courtyard and without a word being spoken communicated that it was time for her to move forward and find her own path now that she was on her own. She was filled with a deep joy, calm and hope for the future as she was flooded with love pouring into her from the being.

After Francis moved away, Patrick and Brian asked about buying Robert's interest in the center. He discussed this with Roberta and Francis, and they all agreed this would be best. He had hesitated at first because he felt like he was selling Anna's dream, but she appeared to him as he drifted off to sleep and told him it was time to let the past be past. He contacted the attorney the following day.

Roberta visited her father and Edna often and began to attend church again. She had attended the church with Lilith when she was very young, but the drive had been so long from the center that they stopped going. Now, as she became involved, she felt a spiritual awakening and discovered she had abilities she had been unaware of. She studied and became increasingly sensitive to her surroundings and to others realizing that she had the same ability to heal as her mother and Francis.

Roberta was very busy with church and writing and practicing her music in preparation for the next record. She volunteered at hospitals and places in the community in order to use her new found abilities to help others. She sought out Robert one day when a young woman she had tried to heal died and she began to doubt that she really had any ability at all. Robert explained that healing is not the same thing as curing and no one can interfere when the time has come for a person to leave this world because this is part of the plan that is made by the soul before we ever enter the body. She also talked to Francis about this and in time was able to understand and detach herself from the outcome when she did healing but just allow the energy to be used in whatever way was best for the person involved whatever the result.

During this time she met and dated a few men but never felt anything special for any of them, and she enjoyed the time she spent with her friends at the bar more than dating. It was more than six months before she felt they were ready to make the next record, and, despite Mr. Hanson's prodding, she refused to be rushed. Her second record was an even bigger success than the first, and she received many invitations to perform and requests for interviews. In the beginning, she was flattered but after a year of not being able to go anywhere without someone wanting something she longed to be anonymous. She was no longer able to go to the bar and sing with Troy and Branden and had to rent a secure place for them to practice. She had a high wall built around the house and was very grateful for the privacy afforded by the courtyard. She still did volunteer work, but had to make certain that she wasn't followed whenever she went out. She longed for the time when the final record was done so that she could take a break for a while.

A few months later, while they were recording the third record, Mr. Hanson mentioned a young man who had come looking for her when she had been in town working on the second record. She knew from the description it was Jaime and was tempted to go to the pub but felt a vague urging that told her this would be the wrong thing to do. When the third record was completed, she refused to sign another contract but promised Mr. Hanson that she would contact him and no one else when she was ready to make another recording.

Christmas had always been a very big event at the center, but since they had left the country it had been a quiet affair at Edna and Robert's home with just her family, Francis and Roberta. Francis called from Chicago a week before Christmas to say he wouldn't be able to make it home for the holidays. Tears filled her eyes as Roberta remembered the Christmases of her childhood and she felt depressed at the thought of spending the day with only her father and strangers she had nothing in common with. Two days before Christmas Edna called late at night to tell her that her father was in the hospital after a heart attack and was not expected to live. She rushed to the hospital and arrived barely in time to say goodbye before he slipped away, and she watched as his spirit floated out of the body and joined Anna and Diana. They all turned and smiled at her before fading away, and Roberta felt loneliness deeper than she had ever imagined possible. She knew that Robert had been very lonely for those who understood and shared his values and visions. Even though Edna was very nice she didn't understand the spiritual things he had shared with Anna, Lilith and the others at the healing center before it became so commercial.

Judy and Hank came as soon as they got the news and stayed until after the funeral. They apologized for having to leave so soon, but she had two children and had to get back to take care of them, and Hank had to get back to work. Francis arrived in time for the funeral and stayed with her for three days before returning to Chicago. When everyone had left and she was alone for the first time, she went into the courtyard and began to cry overcome by loneliness and the void caused by the loss of everyone dear. A bright light suddenly illuminated the courtyard, and she looked up to see a huge, beautiful angel floating just over the pool. The angel moved toward her, and as she was enfolded in its wings, she was filled with peace and incredible love.

Edna invited her to visit any time and called daily to talk to her for a while. Her friends from the bar expressed concern when she said she wanted to just be alone to write her music and paint because she couldn't tell them about the angel. She continued with her church, volunteer work, and music and began to paint more and settled into a comfortable routine. The gnome always sat with her when she wrote her music, and her mother's presence was with her when she painted, and for the first few weeks her father often appeared briefly.

Chapter 12

It had been quite a while since her last record and people had stopped hounding her so much. She was relieved to find that she was able to go to the bar again. She had been practicing a new piece of music with Troy and Branden one night when she looked up to see a man who appeared to be in his early 30s watching from a table in a dimly lit corner of the bar. He approached her just as she was packing to leave and said he just wanted to tell her how much he had enjoyed her playing and singing. She glanced up, and looked into deep blue eyes that seemed to draw her into them. She dropped the case she had been putting her lap harp into, and their hands touched as they both reached to pick it up. An electric shock ran through her body at the touch, and she felt like a clumsy schoolgirl as her face flushed a deep red. He handed her the case and turned to leave as she stammered a thank you.

Two nights later when she returned to the bar, the man was sitting at the same table, and Troy told her he had been there the night before but had left early. They practiced for a while and when they sat down to take a break the man came over, introduced himself as Colin Ryan and asked if he could join them. Troy made room for him at the end of the table across from Roberta, and he asked about the music that they had been playing. He had a very strong Irish accent, and the musical sound of his voice brought back memories of the time she had spent in Ireland. She blushed as the others explained to him that she wrote the music and he complimented her on her wonderful gift. He asked if he could look at her harp because he had never seen one like it before. He laid it across his legs and after a few chords began to play some standard Irish songs. They all joined in and were soon having a wonderful time singing and dancing.

He came to the bar every night after that and played and sang with them, and Roberta's heart sank when she learned that he would be returning to Ireland as soon as he finished his business in a few weeks. As she was leaving the bar one night, Colin walked out with her carrying the cases she kept her music and lap harp in. He put the cases on the seat of the car and then before she realized what was happening took her in his arms and kissed her long and deep before stepping away and turning to go back in the bar. Roberta stood stunned and unable to move until he turned at the door and tipped his hat. She threw herself into the car with her cheeks flushed deep red and backed quickly out of the parking lot almost hitting another car.

The following night she arrived at the bar before Colin did, and everyone began teasing her about the kiss. She was furious when Colin came in, and she stormed over to confront him only to find herself in his arms once more. If he had released her after the kiss, she would have fallen because her knees were so weak, but he kept his arm firmly about her waist as everyone began to whistle and cheer. She turned and drew back her arm to slap him but stopped when she saw the look in his eyes. He told her that he didn't have time to play games because he had to leave the following week and wanted her to marry him and return with him to Ireland. Roberta had never met anyone like him and wasn't sure what to do. She hesitated to take such a chance without knowing anything about him but the thought of never seeing him again was unthinkable.

After having a beer with her friends, the two of them returned to her house and sat talking late into the night, as he told her about his home in Ireland and his family. He promised that she would always be free to be her own person and pursue her music because he loved the person she was and would never try to change her. She knew the time had come when she had to tell him about the special gift she and other members of her family had and their beliefs. As she talked about the things she believed and saw, she watched for some sign that he was upset but saw none. He asked a few questions, and when she had finished he said he had known from the beginning that there was something very special about her. He then told her that his grandmother had always said she saw the little people, but no one had really believed her.

She promised to give him her answer the next day, and when he had left, she sat in the courtyard having a cup of tea before bed and trying to decide what she should do. She looked up to see her parents standing across the courtyard and as they began to fade away she heard her mother whisper that love is too precious to risk losing. She was waiting for Colin when he came into the bar the next night, and when she said she would marry him, he swung her around until she was dizzy. She contacted the attorney the next day to make arrangements for him to take care of everything and gave him the address where she would be. She tried to reach Francis to give him the news but was unable to reach him. They would be leaving in four days, and Colin returned to the house with her to call Francis. When she told him she was to be married in three days, Francis said he couldn't possibly get away on such short notice. Roberta told him she understood and would miss him, and he promised to come visit as soon as he could get away.

That night Colin told her that he didn't want their first time to be on a crowded ship and led her to the courtyard where he had spread sheets over a thick padding of blankets. They made love under the stars and then fell asleep to wake a few hours later and make love again. Roberta marveled at the sensuality he awakened in her. She had wondered if she was cold when she heard other women talk about sex because she had never felt the things they talked about, but she knew now that was certainly not the case. He returned each evening to stay with her, and they went to the bar for a while each evening before returning to the house where they talked late into the night getting to know each other and then fell asleep in each other's arms. When he left each day, she would begin to wonder if she was making a mistake, but as soon as he walked through the door all doubts fled.

All of her friends from the bar were there when they took their marriage vows and to wave as the ship sailed out of the harbor. They stood at the rail watching the land grow ever smaller, and Colin put his arm around her comfortingly as tears flowed from her eyes at the thought of leaving home perhaps forever. They hit rough weather the second day out, and Roberta longed for some of her father's remedy for seasickness. Once the weather calmed down she was fine and enjoyed sitting on the deck with Colin while he talked about his family and his life in Ireland. Colin had sent a letter before they left informing his family of his marriage and that they would be visiting as soon as they returned to Ireland. She was nervous at the thought of meeting his parents and sisters and was glad that they were to have a few days alone before having to face this.

Chapter 13

As the beautiful, green land rose from the sea, she had the same feeling of coming home that she had experienced before. Her pulse quickened with excitement at the prospect of her life in this beautiful country with the wonderful man at her side. The ship arrived on Tuesday, but he had to take care of some business before they could leave toward the end of the week to visit his family for a couple of days. Colin's family home was on the west coast, but he worked for a large firm in Dublin and had a small flat in town. His flat was very cramped, dreary and none too clean, and he told her that she should start looking for something more suitable as soon as they returned from the visit. She spent the time while he worked cleaning and getting things in order and promised herself that she would find something else very quickly.

The drive to the west coast reminded her of all that was wonderful about Ireland. The weather had grown quite chilly, but the scenery stirred deep feelings of belonging that she could not understand and everywhere she looked were elementals, fairies and angels. She began to feel a deep urge to paint again and knew that she would never be bored here. Colin turned off the road and drove through a very impressive gate, and she caught her breath at the natural beauty of the estate as they drove across a bridge toward a modest house built of wood and stone of the area.

As the car pulled to a stop, the front door opened and a middle-aged man and woman hurried toward them. As Colin embraced his mother and kissed her on the cheek and then turned to embrace his father, Roberta found herself suddenly missing her family. Colin drew her to his side and put his arm around her as he introduced her to first his mother Kate, who gave her a kiss on the cheek with a large smile and said she looked forward to getting to know her, and then to his father Sean, who kissed her on both cheeks and gave her a mighty hug as he welcomed her to the family. Colin's two sisters were out for the day, as they had not expected them until later, but they would return in time for dinner. Kate took Roberta's arm and led her into a very pleasant, comfortable room where a fire burned brightly in the fireplace. Roberta quickly relaxed as Colin and his parents talked and they told her stories about Colin's childhood. When his sisters Megan and Claire returned, they both squealed with delight and hurled themselves in Colin's arms nearly knocking him off his feet and then quickly turned to embrace Roberta with the same exuberance and welcomed her to the family.

There was much joking and teasing and by the time they went to bed that night, Roberta felt as though she had known these happy, loving people for years. She snuggled into Colin's arms feeling safe and content as she drifted off to sleep to dream of running across a rich green landscape with elementals and flying through the air with fairies and angels. She had never been with people so energetic and happy before. They played games, laughed, teased, and chased each other, and the days flew by. When the time came to return to Dublin Roberta felt as though she was leaving her own family and was very glad they would be close enough to visit often.

The day after they returned to town, she found a realtor and began looking at properties each day while Colin was at work. The first few days she spent looking at large, pretentious estates that held no interest at all for her. She finally told the realtor that she didn't want to look at anything like what he had been showing her and on the second day he took her to several places that were in line with what she wanted but just not quite right. She sensed the realtor's growing impatience but felt driven to keep looking. He finally told her he had only one more place but was sure that she would not want it because it was quite far out of town and quite run down. It was mid afternoon, and she sensed his reluctance to waste time driving so far and asked if she could look at the property on her own. With obvious relief he gave her directions and the keys and dropped her at Colin's office to get the car.

When she asked Colin about using the car to go look at the house, he decided to take the rest of the day and go with her. He had been working long hours, and they felt like children skipping school as they drove through the countryside with her snuggled in the shelter of his arm. They had driven for quite some time, and Colin was sure they must be lost when they finally saw the sign where they were to turn. As they turned onto the road leading to the property, Roberta was reminded of Lilith telling about the day she and Anna had looked at the property where Roberta grew up, and she sat up to look around. The road curved to reveal a small stone cottage, and she knew that she had found her home. As the car came to a stop, Colin said there was no need to even get out. The cottage was overgrown with vines that tumbled through the damaged roof, and he wondered aloud why the realtor had given her a key since the door hung open held only by a single hinge. She felt compelled to go inside against Colin's protests, and as they approached the door, Roberta saw elementals peeking out from behind the plants with sad looks as though imploring her to buy the place. The gloom inside was relieved by light filtered though the overgrown vines, and Roberta was not at all surprised to see her mother, father and sister standing across the room as though to welcome her home.

On the drive back to town she pleaded as Colin listed all the reasons for not buying the house but could offer no rebuttal except that she knew she belonged there. The following day when she returned the keys to the realtor, she asked the price in spite of the fact that she had been unable to persuade Colin to even consider it. The price was considerably lower than they had expected, and the realtor admitted that the house had been on the market for some time and the owner wanted to sell it. She broached the subject of the house immediately after dinner, and a heated argument ensued with neither of them willing to give in. Roberta admitted that Colin's arguments had merit, but he refused to even listen when she tried to explain that she just knew she was meant to live in that house. She told him about seeing her parents and sister in the cottage and the elementals' imploring eyes and was very hurt when he made comments about her overactive imagination.

For the next week Roberta continued to look at other properties but found nothing that she liked. Colin accused her of being a spoiled American and stated that no good Irish wife would ever behave the way she was doing, and this led to a serious argument during which she told him if he had wanted a good Irish wife that is what he should have married. He stormed out of the house to return very late and go to bed without saying goodnight. Roberta had cried herself to sleep but woke when he came in and lay awake until almost daylight trying to find a solution for this problem that threatened to destroy her marriage before it ever really began. She finally fell asleep to dream about the cottage fully repaired and knew that she had to buy it regardless of what Colin said.

That weekend they visited his family who sensed immediately that there was a problem, and that evening while Kate and Roberta were alone in the kitchen after dinner, Kate asked if Roberta wanted to talk about what was wrong. Roberta found it very difficult to explain her stand without explaining why it was so important, so she told Kate that the members of her family had an unusual ability to know what was right for them. She explained that they all had the ability to see things that others couldn't. She was deliberately vague, but Kate asked for specifics and it was too late to turn back, so Roberta found herself telling everything about her family. As she talked about her family's gifts, she watched Kate's face but was unable to determine what she was thinking. When she had finished explaining, Kate put her arms around Roberta and pulled her close as she patted her on the back and then led her back to sit with the men in the other room. It was obvious that Colin had been talking to his father about the same subject as they stopped talking when the two women entered the room. The four of them talked about general subjects until time for bed and then retired to their beds where both Roberta and Colin lay awake on opposite sides of the bed most of the night.

The next day was gloomy and damp, but Kate asked Colin to go for a walk with her while Roberta talked to his father Sean. Sean said Colin had told him about the property and his objections, which seemed legitimate, and Kate had told him her reasons for wanting the property. Sean then led her to a portrait of a beautiful woman that hung in the hallway and explained that this was his mother who had also had the gift of seeing and knowing things that others couldn't. They talked about Sean's mother and the family until Colin and his mother returned. Roberta never knew what Colin's mother said to him, but when they returned, he walked to Roberta, took her in his arms and gave her a kiss that left her weak and very flushed. The four of them talked for a long time and a solution was finally reached. Colin didn't have the money to pay for the cottage and the repairs, but Roberta had more than enough from Lilith and her father. Since the drive would be much too long for Colin to make each day, he would pay for a modest place in town where they would stay from Monday to Friday and spend the weekends at the cottage once it was repaired enough. Roberta would need her own car so that she could drive to the house on Friday morning where Colin would join her after work, and she could drive back and forth during the week. That night they once again fell asleep in each other's arms after making love and woke before dawn to make love again. Colin jokingly suggested that they have fights often because it was so much fun making up but turned serious and agreed when she said she never wanted them to be angry at each other like that again. This had taught them both how precious love is and how easily it can be lost.

Chapter 14

They returned home on Sunday and Roberta was at the realtor's office when he opened the following morning. They went over all the details of the property and she made an offer that was quite a bit less than the asking price. The realtor said he would present the offer to the owner and contact Colin at his office with the answer. Colin called that afternoon to tell her that their offer had been accepted, and he was taking the remainder of the afternoon off so that they could buy her a car. Roberta would have preferred a different car than that chosen by Colin, but she voiced no objection, as this wasn't worth risking another argument.

On the way out to the cottage, they stopped at a house about a mile away to inquire about someone local to do the repairs and were directed to another house a short distance past the cottage. Colin talked to a man and returned to the car to say that he would meet them at the cottage shortly to talk about the repairs. As the car came to a stop in front of the cottage, Colin turned to look at Roberta and with a wide grin said love must have made him completely daft to agree to this. Roberta kissed him and then jumped laughing from the car as he made a grab for her.

As they began a list of things that would have to be done, only the look on Roberta's face kept Colin from complaining about the money being thrown away. As he watched her pick her way through the rubble, the shafts of sunlight gave her an almost other worldly glow, and for a moment he felt himself being caught up in the spell of the cottage.

When the man Colin had talked to earlier arrived, they introduced themselves and then spent more than an hour discussing what needed to be done and the best way to begin. Roberta stressed that the integrity of the house must be preserved as much as possible. The house had one larger main room with two smaller rooms to the right and one small room in the back. A portion of the back room on the right would be used to build a bathroom, which would leave a small room for a second bedroom, and the front side room would be a large kitchen. The back room would be their bedroom, and Roberta loved the fact that the early morning sun would shine through the windows at the back of the room. They made arrangements to meet Mr. Murphy back at the house in two weeks to get a list of supplies that would be needed, and he would begin work as soon as these were delivered. On the drive back to town that day, Roberta snuggled next to Colin as they talked about the wonderful weekends they would share in the tiny cottage.

She found a small but comfortable apartment on the outskirts of Dublin that was close to his office and only just over an hour from the cottage. They were soon settled into their new home with work underway on the cottage. She often drove out to the cottage as soon as he left for work in the morning always making sure to be back in time to have a meal ready when he returned in the evening. They discovered a small pub around the corner from their apartment and went there many nights to play music and sing. She took her paints and musical instruments whenever she went to the cottage, and it was as though she drew inspiration from the very ground there. She felt her mother's presence very strongly whenever she was painting, and was amazed herself at the results she achieved. Her music also seemed to thrive in the atmosphere of the cottage, and the pieces she composed had a quality that seemed to speak to all that was good in those who heard them. On the weekends, she and Colin often drove to the cottage to eat a picnic lunch and then lie on the grass or work on a piece of music together.

They were both very strong willed, and it was inevitable that disagreements would arise, but they had learned their lesson well and managed to avoid situations that would endanger their relationship. Roberta knew this was the kind of love her father and mother had shared and understood why her father had been so happy to leave this world to rejoin her mother. She often saw them at the cottage and felt closer to them than she ever had. They were visiting Colin's parents when Roberta awoke one morning feeling deathly ill and wondering if she had eaten something bad. She spent most of the morning in the bathroom being sick and the mere mention of food was enough to send her running back to be sick again. She finally began to feel better around noon and dressed to join the others for lunch on the terrace. As she walked through the door, Colin ran to take her arm to lead her to a chair and his mother and father looked up with large smiles on their faces. Roberta was puzzled and wondered why they were acting so strangely. Colin saw the puzzled look on her face and remarked as he bent to kiss her on the forehead that she had better make certain the smaller bedroom of the cottage was made ready for a new addition.

Roberta's eyes widened as she realized what he meant, and her hands flew to protectively cradle her still flat stomach as she absorbed the wonder of what was happening. After lunch, Colin's mother took her to a storage room where they spent the rest of the day sorting through baby clothes and toys, and Roberta and Colin returned home on Sunday with boxes full of things for the baby.

Chapter 15

Roberta had written many songs and had done more than two-dozen paintings, and she talked to Colin about wanting to return to The States to make a record and sell some of her paintings. She would soon be too far along in the pregnancy to travel, and after the child was born it would be a long time before she would be able to make the trip. She had contacted both Mr. Hanson and the owner of the gallery in New York and they were both eager for her to come. Colin was unable to get away long enough to go with her, but she assured him that she would be fine, and he finally agreed to her making the trip. She contacted Francis, and they arranged to meet at Lilith's old house, visit their friends at the center and spend some time together before she went to make the record with Mr. Hanson.

She stood at the railing long after she could no longer see Colin standing on the shore. She had the strange feeling that she had left a part of herself behind and realized that she already missed Colin. As her new homeland was lost in the mist, she thought about the last time she had stood like this with her father and Lilith and suddenly felt very alone. The weather was beautiful, so she spent most of her days on deck putting the final touches on some of her music. The captain had asked her to play for the passengers, so she spent most evenings playing the music that she planned to record in order to get an idea which pieces might be best received. Although the crossing was uneventful, it seemed to take forever and she was eager to see land once again.

The ship docked mid afternoon, and Roberta got a taxi to take her to the hotel where she had stayed with her father and Lilith. She relaxed overnight and arrived at the gallery very early the next morning. She had arranged for the crates of paintings to be delivered, and Mr. Logan was very quiet as the paintings were unpacked, and he walked among them. He finally came to stand beside Roberta and told her that he was very happy with the quality of her paintings. She had done many paintings of the cottage with elementals, fairies and angels, and he seemed quite mesmerized by these. He remarked that it would be wonderful to live in such a perfect place and was surprised when she told him this was her home. She spent most of that day with Mr. Logan as they went through the paintings, and he finally offered to buy all of them for a very generous price. She thanked him when he invited her to have dinner with him and his wife but said she planned to catch a night train home in order to have as much time as possible with her brother, so he offered his car to take her back to her hotel and then to the train station. This would allow her to catch the train that would be leaving at 4 p.m., so she returned to the hotel to quickly clean up and change before leaving for the station.

She arrived very late the next evening and managed to get a car to take her to the house she had shared with Francis and her father after they moved into town. When the door to the courtyard swung open, she saw that a light was on in the living room and realized how much she had missed Francis. He was asleep on the sofa when she came in, and she stood for a while just enjoying being in his presence once again. As though he sensed her presence, Francis opened his eyes, and they quickly moved to embrace each other. They sat up most of the night talking and slept until afternoon of the following day. As they sat having a leisurely cup of tea sitting by the pool the next morning, she was surprised when he asked when her child was due. It had been a long time since she had been with someone who felt the things she did, and she suddenly realized how much she had missed being able to share this.

She told him about the cottage she and Colin had bought, and excusing herself went to her room and returned with a small painting of the cottage that she had painted for him. Francis told her that he was becoming discontent with being a doctor because he felt that he was only treating symptoms and not really helping people the way that he wanted to. He said he was considering moving but had not decided where he wanted to go yet. As Roberta talked about Ireland and the people there, Francis became intrigued and said he might go back with her for a visit when she returned. Roberta was thrilled at the thought of being able to share her beloved Ireland with Francis and urged him to join her. That afternoon they met with the attorney to take care of some business details. The house where they were staying was beginning to be run down again with no one living there, and they had discussed selling it but were both reluctant to lose this last physical tie to their former life.

When they left the attorney's office, Roberta suggested they drive out to the center for a visit since it might be a long time before she was here again. The property had been cleared completely with very few trees left, the private pool had been opened and the stream dammed so that there was now a fairly large lake, and the house and cabins where they had lived had been torn down to make way for a large building. Without even stopping, Francis turned the car around and headed back toward town. They were silent for most of the ride back both lost in their own thoughts and memories, but after a while they began to share the things that they remembered about the wonderful life they had enjoyed at the center. That night they sat in the courtyard and talked about the things their parents had taught them. They agreed that it was time to let go of the past and move on with their lives and decided to contact the attorney the following day and have him sell the house that had belonged to Lilith.

That night they went to the bar where Roberta had met Colin and had a wonderful time with her friends. Troy and Branden were still there, and Roberta asked if they would be able to go accompany her to record the music. Roberta had brought her music with her and as they began to play a hush fell over the bar, as the music seemed to cast a spell over everyone there. When they had finished the first piece, Francis told her the music sounded as though it had come from another world. After playing the music, Troy and Branden both said they would find a way to accompany her. Francis and Roberta had three days together before she had to leave to meet with Mr. Hanson and each night they went to the bar where Roberta practiced with Troy and Branden. She was very busy with Francis and her friends, but she missed Colin and each night the empty bed seemed more and more lonely. As she drifted off to sleep, she seemed to be aware of something connecting the two of them, and it was as though she could feel his very presence in the stillness of the night.

She and Francis spent a great deal of time sitting in the courtyard talking, and they often saw their mother, father, Diana, and Lilith. They both had mixed emotions about selling the house but felt that it was time to make a clean break and there was no reason for them to ever return to this town. They visited Edna to say goodbye and thank her for the happiness she had brought their father.

Francis felt more and more pulled to visit Ireland as he spent time with Roberta and her friends listening to the music and them talking about Ireland. When Roberta left to meet with Mr. Hanson, Francis and Roberta arranged to meet in New York City, and he returned to resign his job at the hospital. Branden and Troy accompanied Roberta, and they spent three days practicing and selecting the pieces to be recorded. They had not played together for quite a while, and the music was very different, so it took two weeks for them to complete the recording to everyone's satisfaction. Roberta had brought much more music, and Mr. Hanson pleaded with her to record more, but she refused. They finished mid afternoon, and Roberta said goodbye to her friends after inviting them to visit her in Ireland and managed to catch the train to New York City that night. She called Francis to let him know that she was leaving, and he said he was catching a train early the following morning, so he would arrive shortly after she did.

She spent the night in the observation car dosing and waking to watch as the train sped past farms and towns. It was late the following day when the train pulled into the station, and Roberta was very tired when she reached the hotel. She went to bed after taking a hot bath and having a light snack sent up to the room. The last two weeks had been very draining, and she looked forward to doing only what she wanted to do. The following morning she had breakfast sent to her room and just enjoyed the luxury of having nothing to do. Francis arrived that afternoon, and they sat in the room talking until time to go to dinner.

The next day Roberta took Francis to the gallery to see her paintings. When they arrived, Mr. Logan hurried over to tell her that her paintings were selling as fast as he could get them hung. He took them to the back where the remainder of the paintings were being framed and prepared for hanging. As Francis stood looking at the paintings, he felt a stirring deep within and knew that his decision to accompany Roberta back to Ireland had been right. He told Roberta that he felt a sense of expectation and excitement and knew that his life was going to move in a wonderful new direction.

They boarded the ship the next day and strolled the decks becoming acquainted with other passengers and finding their way around. Fortunately, Roberta had asked Francis about getting something for seasickness, so they enjoyed the crossing despite turbulent weather and seas that were quite rough. They both preferred the open deck even when the wind blew the salt spray to cover them in a gritty layer. Roberta found herself more and more restless, and the last night she had difficulty sleeping in anticipation of seeing Colin again. Once again, she took blankets and slept on deck to be certain of catching the first glimpse of her beloved Ireland, and Francis joined her. They both dosed off and on and just as dawn was breaking she shook Francis awake. They stood at the railing together as the land grew closer and closer. It was shrouded in mist and looked very much like a fairytale scene, and Francis seemed to be caught in its spell. They went inside only long enough to grab some food to take back on deck and spent the hours until they docked lost in their private thoughts.

Chapter 16

As the ship slipped into its berth, Roberta finally caught sight of Colin and tears of joy filled her eyes. She had sent him a letter telling him when she would arrive and that Francis was coming with her, but the ship had arrived early, and she had not expected him to be here. As soon as the gangplank was in place, she ran down it and threw herself into her husband's arms. They kissed with all the pent up emotions of their separation totally oblivious of those around them. Many of the other passengers expressed their disapproval at such disgraceful behavior, but Colin and Roberta were unaware of anything except each other. Francis had stayed to take care of their luggage and then joined them on the dock. Roberta laughed as he cleared his throat to get their attention and moved out of Colin's embrace to stand nestled beside him while she introduced them. Her cheeks were flushed, and Francis envied her the love that shone so obviously from both their eyes as she and Colin stood close together.

There wasn't enough room in their flat for Francis, and Colin had arranged for a room in the house next door for him. After dropping off the luggage, the three of them went to the local pub where they talked, played music and sang for a couple of hours. Roberta asked about the cottage and Colin told her that it was in good enough condition for them to stay there. The next day was Friday and Colin had arranged to take the day off, so they made plans to drive out to the cottage for the weekend. Francis was tired and he knew that Colin and Roberta longed to be alone, so he suggested they retire early. They said goodnight and retired to their beds where Roberta and Colin made love and fell asleep to wake before dawn to make love again and then sit watching the sunrise while they talked about how much they had missed each other and all that had happened since they were last together.

Roberta woke Francis early the next morning eager to have breakfast and be on their way to the cottage. They stopped long enough to buy food and the other necessities before leaving town, and once back in the car Roberta snuggled next to Colin happier than she had ever thought she could be. It was an overcast day with a chill in the air, and Francis shivered as they drove through the countryside. They were all quiet as Francis and Roberta drank in the mystical beauty of this land, and Colin was content just to have the most important person in his life back with him.

When they turned onto the road leading to the cottage, Roberta sat up in anticipation. Colin had pushed everyone to work very hard to get everything in shape while she was gone, and as the cottage came into view, Roberta stared in surprise. All of the flowers, bushes and trees around the cottage had been trimmed to bring them into control and were filled with a riot of brilliantly colored blooms. She was speechless with the beauty of the place and almost caused Colin to wreck the car when she turned to throw her arms around his neck and kiss him with great fervor. When the car stopped, she stood with her arms open as though to take it all into herself. Francis stood in awe and said a prayer of thanksgiving for having this special place with these two wonderful people. He had been unaware how starved his soul was until this moment and now he felt a rebirth of the desire to heal and help that had been so much of part of his life when he was young. The three of them spent the weekend roaming the countryside, playing music and singing while the magic of the place restored them. Roberta's hands were never still as she was either playing music or painting in every spare moment.

As they sat outside watching the sun sink low on the horizon the last evening before they were to return to town, their attention was drawn to a spot a short distance away where Anna, Robert, Diana, Lilith, and another woman that Roberta thought looked familiar appeared and then slowly faded away. Roberta turned to find Colin ashen and visibly shaken as he pointed unable to speak. Roberta and Francis both hurriedly assured him that everything was fine. They explained that it was just their parents, sister, friend and a lady they didn't know. Once Colin was able to speak, he told them that the other lady had been his grandmother. Roberta remembered the painting Colin's father had shown her of his mother and realized this was why the woman had seemed familiar. Colin was quite shaken by the experience and said he would just as soon not see things like that anymore while Roberta and Francis talked about it being a gift to be able to see those we love after they have passed and how comforting it is to know that they are not really gone.

They all returned to town early the next morning where Colin went to work and Roberta and Francis sat talking over a cup of coffee. Francis told Roberta that he thought he might stay in Ireland and find a way to use his medical and natural healing abilities again the way he knew he was meant to. He said he had not felt so inspired since he left the center to go away to college. They discussed living arrangements, and he said he would like to find something in the vicinity of the cottage so that they could be close and perhaps work together. Roberta took him to see the realtor she had dealt with and left him there while she did some shopping before returning home to prepare dinner. That evening over dinner, Francis filled them in on his search for a house. Roberta was very happy to know that Francis was staying. Colin really liked Francis and was relieved to know that they would have a doctor close by when the time came for Roberta to give birth. She was starting to show now, and he liked running his hands over her swollen stomach.

Colin had promised his parents they would visit the second weekend after Roberta returned, so they threw everything in the car and left as soon as Colin got home from work on Friday. Roberta had fixed food that they could eat while they drove, and they enjoyed the picnic type atmosphere. Francis had protested when they invited him to come along feeling that he would be in the way but gave in when both Colin and Roberta insisted. They pointed out that he could help drive home Sunday night, which would allow Colin to get some sleep and allow them to have a longer visit. There was a full moon that night, and Roberta and Francis both lost themselves in the lushness and beauty of the countryside. They spoke in hushed voices about how they felt and pointed out the elementals along the way to each other. Francis asked Colin about the history of Ireland and they listened as he told them how the Irish had suffered under English rule and finally managed to regain their country. Colin told them about the potato famine that had been the cause of mass immigrations to the United States.

The car had barely stopped when Colin's entire family came out to welcome Anna home. Colin introduced Francis while Anna was hugged vigorously by each of them. Amid much laughter and teasing, the group filed back into the living room where a welcoming fire burned brightly. Francis took a chair close to the fire grateful for its warmth as the air had turned quite chilly and he had not had time to adjust to the damp, cool climate. Even though it was quite late, they sat talking and stuffing themselves with the food that Colin's mother and sisters had prepared well into the night and went to bed very tired and contented. It rained the following day, and everyone stayed indoors playing games and talking. Roberta told them about her trip, selling her paintings and her recording session. She said that even though she enjoyed seeing her old friends, she had felt homesick and longed to return to Ireland. Francis told them that he was thinking of staying in Ireland and starting a medical practice, and he and Sean talked about the laws and business details he would need to address in order to open a practice. Megan and Claire both vied for Francis' attention and seemed very happy to hear that he was thinking of staying, but Francis seemed oblivious to their attention and only interested in talking business.

On Sunday they went to the local church after which the girls invited Francis to go horseback riding. He accepted happy to be able to get out and see the surrounding area while Colin, Roberta, Kate and Sean discussed everyday things. They talked about a name for the baby and Kate mentioned that her father's mother had been named Tressa. Roberta really liked that name, so they agreed that if the child were a girl she would be named Tressa Anne. The others continued to talk about names for a boy and Roberta joined in, but she had known almost from the beginning that she was carrying a girl. After dinner, the car was loaded and everyone walked out with them to say goodbye. Before leaving they arranged for Colin's family to join them at the cottage whenever they were able to get away for the weekend.

Colin drove for a while and then stretched out in the back seat to sleep while Roberta and Francis sat talking about the past, Ireland and Colin's family. Francis was more determined than ever to stay in Ireland and eager to get settled into a new life here. Colin listened as they talked about their childhood, and he dreamed of living in a world of magic full of fairies, gnomes and all manner of wondrous things. In his dream, he again saw his grandmother and this time instead of being afraid, he was happy to be able to spend time with her and relive the happiness they had enjoyed together when he was young.

Chapter 17

In the weeks that followed, Roberta spent as much time as possible at the cottage working on the house and grounds and Colin began to worry that she was doing too much for someone in her condition. They talked about this, and Roberta tried to explain that whatever she did in the house or on the grounds seemed to give her strength and improve her health, but Colin continued to worry, so she forced herself to cut back and did not talk so much about what she did.

There had always been fresh foods at the center when she was growing up, and she had missed this since leaving there. One night, as she and Colin were enjoying a quiet evening at home, she broached the subject of hiring someone to farm the land at the cottage in order for them to have fresh food. Colin resisted until she pointed out how much better it would be for them and that it would provide them with good fresh food at virtually no cost, as after the initial outlay they would just take a share of the food in exchange for use of the land and equipment. Colin was a shrewd businessman, and he agreed providing she not try to do the work herself. The following day she drove out to talk to Mr. Murphy about finding someone to farm the land. He told her he would ask around and let her know the next time she came out, and she returned to spend some time at the cottage before returning to town where she sat outside in the warm sun watching the elementals, doing some simple sketches and playing the lap harp.

Francis had bought a car and asked for permission to stay at the cottage most of the time while he looked for property in the area. He had exhausted all the prospects of the realtors in town and said he felt he should just wander around on his own until he found the right place. Roberta had been hoping to spend some time with him that day before she had to leave and was happy to see his car coming up the lane shortly after noon. Francis jumped from the car and ran over to give her a hug and whirled her around before placing her back safely on the ground. He was so excited that Roberta had trouble following what he was saying, but she finally understood that he had found the property that he wanted and wanted her to come with him to see it. He assured her she would have plenty of time to get home early enough to keep Colin from worrying. They decided to leave his car at the cottage since he would be going into town to talk to a realtor, and she and Colin would be coming out the following afternoon for the weekend, so he could just ride back with them.

They made several turns and passed a number of very interesting sites that made Roberta wish she had brought her paints and had time to capture them. She made a note to be prepared the next time she came this way. After almost an hour, Francis pointed out a very old gate that was in need of repair, and she turned onto an overgrown road that led through what had obviously once been well-maintained grounds but was now mostly weeds. They crossed a small stream on a lovely stone bridge and followed the road as it turned left. At first she didn't see the house because it was built of natural materials that seemed to blend into the landscape. As they got closer, she realized that it was much larger than she had first thought and wondered what in the world Francis wanted with such a large house. She stopped the car, and they approached the large double doors that hung open as though inviting them to enter. The entryway was open to the second story and a wide, winding stone staircase gave access to the floor above. There had been much damage done to the house by people, animals and the elements, but it still retained a quiet beauty and dignity that transcended all of that. Roberta voiced concern about the fact that he would be so far out, but Francis assured her that it wasn't as far as she thought. When they reached the road, Francis directed her to turn left, and it took less than an hour to get back into Dublin. There had only been time for a quick tour of the house before they had to leave, but she agreed that it was wonderful.

Francis talked to the realtor the following morning to have him get information about the house, and that afternoon when Colin finished work they all drove to the house before going to the cottage for the weekend. Colin said he remembered hearing something about a house out this way and was sure this was the one, but he couldn't remember what it was he had heard. They stayed for quite some time talking about the possibilities of the house, and it was starting to get dark when they finally decided to leave. They were passing through the hallway when Roberta and Francis both stopped frozen by a sudden sense of foreboding and heaviness. They both turned together to look at the top of the stairs where a hazy figure stood staring down into the hall. Colin turned to see what they were looking at and almost tripped as he ran the rest of the way outside. When Roberta and Francis finally joined him at the car, he was very shaken and said he remembered now hearing that the house was haunted and no one had been able to live there for many years. Rumor had it that the woman who had owned the house was killed there, and she would not allow anyone else to live in her house. That night they talked about this situation and what could be done about it. Roberta was sure that her parents would be able to help, but Francis was not certain since they had passed all the way over and this spirit seemed to be caught between worlds.

Roberta spent the weekend painting and working with Colin on a new piece of music while Francis read and occasionally made suggestions or asked questions, and they all joined in to fix meals and clean up. It was very relaxing, and they returned to town on Sunday night rejuvenated and ready to face another week. Early Monday morning, Francis spoke with the realtor who told him he had found the owner of the house, but he seemed reluctant to talk about it until Francis said they had visited the house over the weekend and had seen the ghost. The realtor then told him that the owner would almost give the house away if Francis was still interested, and Francis said he would let him know in a few days. He went to the library where he found Roberta already searching for books that might help them deal with the situation at the house. They found several books and took them to the desk to check out. When the librarian saw which books they had chosen, she asked if they had experience dealing with things of this nature. Francis explained about the house he wanted to buy, and the woman said she was familiar with it. She warned them that they should be very careful because several people had attempted to stay in the house and never been seen again. She suggested they might want to speak to a lady who lived close by and had experience with this type of thing, and gave them directions to where she lived.

It was getting quite late, and Roberta had to get home to fix dinner, so they said goodbye outside the library. She walked home lost in thought trying to remember all that she had heard about the forces of darkness and how to deal with them. She was concerned that Francis was not taking this seriously enough and worried that he could be hurt. She prepared dinner and sat down to rest while she waited for Colin. She was just starting to dose off when her parents and sister Diana appeared across the room. They told her that there was more than one ghost in the house and that the negative energy was very strong there. They told Roberta that she should not go back into the house until it was cleared because of possible danger to the child she carried but that she could help clear the house without being there by concentrating on sending healing energy to the ghosts and helping them to accept their condition and pass on over.

Francis arrived shortly before Colin got home from work, and Roberta told him what their parents had said. Francis had seen the lady the librarian had suggested, and she had also warned him not to be careless dealing with this. The lady, whose name was Mrs. Warren, said she would be glad to do whatever she could to help Francis and she would contact some of her friends who could also help. Francis was to meet with them the following day, and Roberta planned to go with him. As they ate dinner, Roberta told Colin what her parents had said, and he was very relieved to know that she would not be going back to the house.

Roberta and Francis met with Mrs. Warren and her friends the following morning and plans were made for a group to go to the house a few days later. Roberta really enjoyed meeting Mrs. Warren and her friends and found them to be much like the people she had known growing up. She had been very happy with Colin and their life together and had not realized how much she missed talking to people that she could discuss her beliefs with openly and learn more about the things that were so important to her. Colin had shown increasing concern about her going to the cottage alone as she grew larger, and it was good to have new friends. There was one very shy young woman named Hannah who seemed somehow familiar, and when she mentioned this on the way home Francis remarked that she looked a lot like their mother's friend Sarah whose picture had hung in the living room when they were growing up.

Francis and a group of their new friends went out to the house the following week to try to clear the house. They had gone during the day because it was felt to be safer than night when dark forces are more powerful, but they only succeeded in helping a couple of the lesser forces to cross over. They returned a few days later but were still unable to completely clear the primary dark force, and they finally decided to return at night to deal with this in spite of the danger. They agreed on a time to go so that Roberta and some of the others could help even though they could not be present. That night Roberta sat in deep meditation sending healing, protective energy and was relieved when she realized that her parents were with her. She never knew what happened at the house that night because none of those present would talk to her about it, but the house was finally cleared and Francis bought the house the following day.

Chapter 18

Roberta felt very drawn to Hannah and in the weeks that followed they became close friends doing their shopping together and visiting over cups of tea. Hannah didn't drive, and she was happy not to have to carry heavy bags all of the way home. Since Colin didn't want Roberta going to the cottage alone, she asked Hannah to go with her a couple of times when she went out to see how the farming was progressing and to get away from the city for a while. As they sat outside in the sunshine, Roberta made a sketch of Hannah and then brought out her flute and began to play. Hannah mentioned that she had always wanted to play music but never had a chance to learn. Roberta showed her the basics about the flute and then handed it to her while she went inside to get the harp that she always kept at the cottage. Though she was very hesitant at first, Hannah was comfortable with Roberta and by the end of the day was becoming comfortable with the flute. When the time came to return to town, Roberta insisted that Hannah take the flute with her to practice. It wasn't long before Hannah had mastered the flute and began working with the lap harp.

Colin and Roberta still often visited the pub in the evenings where they worked together writing and playing music. Roberta was happier than she had ever been and the time flew as she eagerly awaited the birth of their child. Colin's family visited them at the cottage on the weekends several times each month, and Francis dropped by every couple of days as the time grew close for her to give birth. During this time, Roberta and Colin grew even closer as they enjoyed the long winter evenings sitting by the fire playing music and talking.

Their daughter was born on a beautiful winter day at the cottage with Colin, his parents and Francis present. Everyone had tried to get Roberta to stay in town when her time grew close, but she stood firm on wanting her child born in the cottage where she knew that they would both have a protection much stronger than any hospital could give, but Colin was relieved to know that Francis would be there should there be any complications. As the time grew close, her mother and father appeared by the bedside and she felt their love close around her to ease the pain. She also saw the angel and the being of light that she had seen before standing at the side of the room and knew that they were there to safeguard her and the child from any harm. The baby immediately let out an ear splitting scream on entering the world and continued this until she was placed in Roberta's arms when she just as suddenly stopped screaming and went to sleep.

Roberta fell into an exhausted sleep with her tiny daughter close at her side, and Tressa Anne stirred sleepily and began sucking on her hand when Colin picked her up to place her in the cradle by the fire. He stood looking down on this perfect little person and felt something deep within him stir as tears of love and joy filled his eyes. Colin took two weeks off, and they stayed at the cottage to give Roberta time to regain her strength. Colin's mother was there to help care for the baby and do the cooking, and Francis stopped by each day to check on the mother and baby, and Colin's father and sisters came out on the weekends.

Francis was living in a small section of his house now while the rest was being repaired, and there had been no further problems with ghosts. Colin's family had never seen the house, and Francis invited them all to join him one Saturday for lunch. Colin was very hesitant to go to the house, but Francis assured him that it was safe, and Roberta was eager to see it once again, so Colin finally agreed. They took both cars because Colin and Roberta planned to return to town that evening. Francis had invited his and Roberta's new friends, so with Colin's family there was a large sized crowd. Roberta was very happy to see Hannah and surprised at how much progress she had made with the music in such a short time. Most of the major repairs had been made, so Francis gave them all a tour of the house that was slowly regaining the beauty it had known before being abandoned. As they toured the house, Roberta noticed that Megan had taken on the role of hostess. She began to notice the special looks that passed between Francis and Megan and how often they managed to find themselves together and smiled as she realized her brother had found someone to love at last.

Roberta and Colin spent most of their evenings at home in town during the week and at the cottage on the weekends just enjoying their family and friends. Hannah came almost every day during the week to practice her music and visit. She wrote lyrics for some of the music that Roberta had written and sang them in her soft lilting voice, which was perfect for the music. Roberta had gotten several letters from Mr. Hanson inquiring about making another recording, but she had been too busy with the baby to think much about it though he had offered to come to Ireland to do the recording. She talked to Hannah about possibly playing and singing and then wrote a letter to Mr. Hanson to let him know that she was working on more music but was not yet ready to record. She also mentioned that she would want to do some vocals the next time.

Roberta found motherhood to be a rewarding though often exhausting job and was glad when it was time to put Tressa to bed and have some time alone with the husband she still adored. Colin was totally captivated by this little creature they had made. He spent hours talking to her while Tressa gurgled and smiled, and he looked forward to her getting older so that she could understand what he was saying. The days passed happily, and though Roberta was very busy, she often stopped to say a silent prayer of thanks for her many blessings.

Chapter 19

Roberta had little interest in politics, but it seemed that the men talked of nothing but Germany and Italy invading more and more countries in Europe, and a sense of dread began to build in Roberta. It was a chilly, wet fall day when the news came that England and France had declared war on Germany. Roberta and Hannah had spent the day finishing a new piece of music, and she rushed to greet Colin as he came home eager to tell him about it. The look on his face was enough for her to know that something was terribly wrong, and she felt as though her happy life had been invaded as he told her the news. That night they went to the pub where the talk centered on the war and speculation about what it would mean for Ireland.

During the rest of 1939 and into the summer of 1940, the news grew increasing worse as country after country was occupied by Germany. When France fell, Germany turned its attention to England, and Colin told Roberta he had to enlist. He enlisted the following morning and was given a week to get his affairs in order before leaving. He had no idea where he would be after he finished training in England, but it was unlikely that he would be back in Ireland very soon. Colin and Roberta decided to give up the place in town, as it would be safer for her and Tressa to be at the cottage. The farm was doing very well now, and they would be more self-sufficient there. They moved everything to the cottage two days later with the help of Francis and his father and mother who had come to see him before he left, and then went back home to allow Roberta and Colin to have the last day for themselves and their daughter. They spent their day playing music and walking across the beautiful landscape talking about the little things that couples share. That night they lay awake reluctant to give up even a moment of their precious time together.

Colin left early the next morning, and Roberta stood watching long after the car had disappeared from view. Finally, she heard Tressa stirring and went inside to fix her breakfast. Roberta was grateful when Francis came over that afternoon to check on them. She had been unable to settle down all day and felt as though her entire life had been jerked away from her. Francis had rented an office in Dublin to set up a practice but was wondering if that would be a good idea. They talked about the war and speculated on the possible ramifications of it. Before he left, they made arrangements to go into town to church on Sunday and see their friends. Roberta felt better after Francis' visit and sat down to work on a new piece of music while Tressa played on the floor.

The days settled into a routine of painting, writing music, taking care of Tressa and the house and eagerly watching for the mail in hopes of getting a letter from Colin. He had been gone for almost two weeks when the first letter arrived, and she held it to her heart as tears flowed down her cheek. He wrote about the training that he was undergoing and the men who were part of his group, but said he still had no idea where he would be going next. As Roberta read the letter she became aware of the sensation she had experienced while in the United States of a cord connecting them. She had been preoccupied with other things before but during this time she became more aware of the elementals, and the gnome often came and sat with her while she painted or played music. She found that she was becoming more sensitive to her surroundings and saw things that she had not noticed before.

Throughout the winter, she went into town a couple of times each week to visit and do shopping. She and Francis went to church on Sundays, and Hannah sometimes came back to the cottage with her so that they could work on the music. When spring came, everyone at the farm was very busy, and Roberta helped out with some of work. It was good to be out in the fresh air again, and she knew that the food would be more important now that their income was less. Of course living expenses were very low at the cottage, and she still had some money coming in from the sale of her records and some from her father's estate, but she had spent a lot of what she had on the cottage and farm.

Hannah came out to stay for a few days and helped out on the farm. She seemed to enjoy the work and since she was not happy with her job, Roberta offered her the opportunity to stay at the cottage and help with the farm. She would only be able to pay her a small amount but since there would be no living expenses she would have as much as she did working in town. This would give them more time to work on the music and Roberta would enjoy the company. Hannah hesitated concerned that Roberta was just being nice, but after being reassured that she would be of help she happily accepted the offer. Francis offered to store some of Hannah's things at his house because the cottage was so small, and many of their friends pitched in to help her move that week.

The two women worked hard on the farm and preserving food that summer and fall, and when winter came the pantry was filled to the rafters. Hannah occasionally stayed in town for a few days in order to give Roberta some time alone with Tressa and to catch up with her friends. When Tressa celebrated her second birthday, Roberta sent Colin a picture of her with cake all over her face. His letters were fewer and usually arrived in groups since he had finished training. He wasn't able to tell her where he was, and she worried whenever she heard of a battle being fought.

She had not heard from him for some time and was beginning to worry one day when the gnome came to sit with her. He always knew what was bothering her and that day when she suddenly arose and began pacing the floor for the third time in an hour, he reminded her that she could always know if Colin was well by quieting herself and focusing on the cord that bound them. Following his instructions, she focused her thoughts and as she sat with closed eyes she became aware of the cord and knew that Colin was well because of the strength of the vibration. She also knew that if he were to die she would no longer be aware of the cord that connected them, and that helped to ease her worry. After this, she took time each day to focus on this connection and to send energy to Colin.

Hannah had been at the cottage for about a month when she rather hesitantly asked if Roberta ever saw things here that she didn't ordinarily see. When asked what she meant, she said that she sometimes caught a glimpse of movement and thought that she had seen some strange little creatures a couple of times. Roberta began to laugh and brought out some of the paintings she had done of the elementals. She explained that everyone in her family saw these little people and that it was certainly not her imagination. They often talked about this other world after that and as Hannah became more accepting she began to see more so that one day as they were working on a piece of music Roberta introduced her to the gnome who had made an appearance.

Roberta felt restless one day and suggested that they go on a picnic while the weather was still warm enough. They packed the car and Roberta decided to take her paints and go to one of the ancient sites she had noticed on the way to Francis' house. They set everything up in a spot close to a cluster of large stones, and Roberta began to paint the landscape. She quickly became lost in her painting as Hannah and Tressa ran and played among the stones. After a couple of hours, Hannah interrupted to suggest they eat, and Roberta, suddenly realizing how late it was, apologized. They sat in the warm sunlight eating and laughing at Tressa who was chasing butterflies and having a wonderful time. Roberta saw Hannah looking intently at the painting she had been working on and looked to see what had caught her interest. She had painted many figures in ancient clothing wandering among the large stones and fairies flying through the air. As she looked at the landscape, she let her eyes become slightly unfocused and suddenly the scene came alive again. She explained to Hannah how to let her eyes relax and become unfocused, and Hannah suddenly took a deep breath as she began to see the people and fairies. They both watched as Tressa walked over to one of the women and began talking to her and then watched as she ran off again playing with the fairies.

That night Roberta told Hannah about growing up at the center and the paintings that her mother did. She explained how she had never believed in these things until she had her own experience with the magical stone cottage. She told Hannah about the fight she and Colin had when she found her cottage because he couldn't understand how important it was to her. Roberta had often wondered why Hannah never seemed to date but had not wanted to pry. Hannah told Roberta that night that she had been very much in love with a young man she had known her entire life. They had planned to marry when they finished school, but he had been killed in an accident. This had been very hard for her, and she had become very solitary after that. They talked about death, and Roberta explained her belief that death was merely a returning home to prepare for the next part of the soul's journey toward perfection. She gave Hannah a couple of books on this subject and over the following weeks they enjoyed many deep discussions about the mysteries of life. Even though Hannah had heard many of these things before, she admitted that she had never really believed until she spent time at the cottage.

Hannah had returned to town for a couple of weeks to spend time with her other friends, and Roberta enjoyed the time she had alone with just her daughter and Francis who stopped by often just to say hello and check on them. The farm was doing very well, and Hannah would be returning soon to help with preserving food for the coming year, but Roberta suspected that she had begun to see someone in town because she was spending more and more time there.

Francis stopped by one day to tell Roberta that he was turning his house into a rehab hospital for allied forces, especially those of the United States. Roberta was surprised to learn that the United States had troops based in Ireland, and as they talked she began to understand the full scope of the war. Francis had not told her much before because she had not wanted to hear about it but now she seemed to want to know everything. Francis had talked to their friends in town about helping the troops during rehab, and they were all excited to be able to do their part, and Roberta said she would help to supply food from the farm and with healing whenever she could.

Hannah returned with Roberta after church Sunday to help with the food preparation and on the way home she confirmed what Roberta had suspected. She thanked Roberta for helping her get past the death of the boy she had loved and be able to love again. She told Roberta she was moving back to town so that she could have more time with her young man whose name was Sean. They talked late into the night and as Roberta saw the joy shining in Hannah's eyes, the longing to have Colin home again became an almost unbearable ache. That night as she prepared for bed, she concentrated on the bond between them but it seemed weak, and it took a long time sending energy before the bond seemed restored. She assumed that her emotions had interfered with her concentration and fell asleep to dream about sitting in the late afternoon watching the sunset with Colin and walking through the countryside with him.

Chapter 20

Life became very busy and the days flew by as the food ripened and had to be preserved or sold. But no matter how exhausted and used up she felt, each night Roberta took time to connect through the bond with Colin. She made excuses to herself at first because the bond seemed to be weakening; however, she became concerned as this continued and she had to spend more and more time sending energy to strengthen the bond once again. On one of the trips to take food to Francis' house for the troops, she sought him out to ask if he could spare a little time even though she knew he was very busy and told him what was happening. Francis told her that he would gather as many of their friends as he could each evening and send energy to help. He didn't try to tell her that there was nothing to worry about because they both knew this could mean that something was wrong and Colin was slipping away.

She had not received a letter from Colin in weeks when the postman delivered an official looking letter. Her hands trembled as she stood holding the letter with tears streaming down her face. Hannah came around the house from the barn with Tressa and stopped short at the sight of Roberta holding the letter. Hannah took Tressa inside, gave her some cookies and a glass of milk and then returned to Roberta's side. She then took the letter that Roberta held out to her, opened it and read the rather curt letter of regret informing her that Colin was missing and presumed dead. Roberta turned without a word and moved across the yard toward the fields. Hannah stood watching her walk away wishing she could help ease Roberta's pain and unsure what to do. She became alarmed as Roberta disappeared from sight and went to the barn to have one of the men saddle a horse

and go after her. It was more than an hour before they returned. The day
had turned cold and rainy, and Roberta sat on the horse behind the man
shivering and staring as though at something unseen. Hannah thanked
the man and then led Roberta into the house, stripped her wet clothes off
and wrapped her in a blanket that had been warming by the fire. Hannah
talked soothingly as she tended to Roberta's physical needs and tried to
reach her emotionally, but Roberta seemed to be lost in a world of her
own. Hannah was unable to get Roberta to eat, so she put her to bed and
returned to sit by the fire to pray for Colin and Roberta. She was startled
when Roberta suddenly appeared and asked if there was anything left to
eat as though it were just a normal day. While Roberta ate, she explained
that she knew Colin was alive but that he may be very ill, and she had to
stay strong in order to help him.

Colin's family had visited whenever they could but with progression of
the war travel had become much more difficult, and it had been several
months since their last visit. Roberta knew that she had to tell them about
Colin and tried several times to write but was unable to find the right
words to tell Kate and Sean that their only son was missing and presumed
dead. She knew that she would be able to explain how she knew he was
alive and decided to make the trip to tell them in person. The following
day she talked to Francis about the trip. He voiced concerns about her
traveling so far alone with Tressa and said he could go with her since all
of the current patients only needed routine care. Although Roberta knew
that his concern for her safety was genuine, she suspected he had his own
reason for wanting to make the trip.

Arrangements were made for one of the doctors from town to check
on the patients from Thursday afternoon until Monday morning. They
arrived on Thursday just as the family was ready to sit down to dinner. Extra
places were hurriedly set for them while Tressa was kissed and hugged by
each in turn, and Francis explained that they had unexpectedly managed
to get some time away. Dinner was a happy event with everyone laughing
and talking at once. Roberta noticed that Megan and Francis barely ate
at all and after dinner they went for a walk while the others settled by the
fire with their coffee. The moment that Roberta had dreaded had finally
arrived, and she was searching for a way to begin when Sean came to stand
beside her chair, put his hand on her shoulder and asked what was the real
reason for her visit. With tears in her eyes, Roberta took the letter from her
purse and silently handed it to Sean who went to where Kate was sitting
so they could read it together. When they had finished reading, Roberta
explained about the connection she felt with Colin and tried to reassure
them by saying she knew Colin was alive because the bond between them
was still intact.

The weekend passed quickly as they got caught up on that was happening with each member of the family. Roberta listened hungrily as Kate and Sean talked about Colin as it seemed to bring him closer. They parted reluctantly with much hugging and kissing on Sunday with plans to spend Christmas together. On the drive home, Francis told Roberta that he and Megan had talked about getting married once things were more settled. They planned to announce their engagement at Christmas. Roberta kissed Francis on the cheek and teasingly assured him that no one was going to be surprised. She was very happy for him and only wished there were no war to complicate things. It was almost dark when they reached the cottage, so she gave Francis a quick kiss on the cheek and carried her sleeping daughter in the house and to bed.

From the day that she received the letter, Roberta began and ended each day in meditation strengthening the bond with Colin. There were many times when she had difficulty connecting, and she would feel a flood of despair wash over her which was replaced by relief when she was finally able to make the connection and feel it grow strong once again. The more time she spent in meditation, the more she opened to the less visible wonderful world around her. Her parents often appeared when she was drifting off to sleep to comfort and encourage her. She saw elementals wherever she looked and was more aware of the energies around her. One morning she finished her meditation and walked outside to watch the sunrise through the early morning mist. As she sat by the door, a bright light formed and a very large figure slowly took shape in the light. She watched as it came closer and saw that it was a beautiful angel. The beauty of the angel's voice filled her with joy, as she was reassured that she was helping Colin by what she was doing. As the sun rose behind the angel, it slowly faded away to be replaced by the light of a new day, and Roberta rose to begin the day with renewed hope for the future.

Chapter 21

The walls of what had been a large storage building stood not far from the cottage, and as the days grew colder and there was less to do on the farm, Roberta had the men do repairs to convert it into living quarters. She had talked to a couple who both worked at the farm about living there. Rose and her husband rented a place a couple of miles away and agreed it would be more convenient if they were closer. The building was large enough to be divided into living quarters for them and their two children with a couple of separate rooms for guests or other workers. This was finished by the holidays, and Rose moved in with her family just before Thanksgiving. Tressa enjoyed having the other children to play with, and Roberta felt more comfortable having people she knew close by. The sound of the children's laughter brightened up the days and Roberta found herself humming more often as she went about the daily business of living.

Francis, Roberta and Tressa visited Colin's family for Christmas. Francis talked to Sean in private on Christmas Eve, and on Christmas day he and Megan announced their engagement and said they had decided to get married in May. The visit was short because many troops had been brought in just before they left, and Francis was badly needed at the rehab hospital, but they left happy knowing they would be returning in May for the wedding.

When Roberta was at home, she and Tressa took long walks and played games, and Tressa often danced when she played music. Roberta spent as much time as possible at Francis' house helping to care for the wounded but left Tressa with Rose because she didn't want her to be exposed to the horrors of war. One day when she arrived at Francis' house she found the house overrun with people and learned that Dublin had been bombed the night before. She remembered hearing noises during the night but had thought it must be distant thunder. Their friends had brought the news when they came to help with the wounded that day, and Francis invited them all to stay at the house because it would be much safer than living in town for now. Roberta immediately sought out Hannah and invited her and Sean to stay with her and Tressa at the cottage.

Everyone worked long hours that day and Roberta was exhausted when she finally reached home. Rose had fed Tressa, put her to bed, and placed a plate of food, which Roberta gratefully accepted, by the fire to keep it warm. Roberta thanked Rose for her help and told her about the city being bombed as she sat down to eat. When Roberta had finished eating, she put the dirty dishes to soak and went to her room to meditate before going to sleep. It was difficult to make the connection because of her fatigue, but she was finally successful and began sending energy to Colin. She suddenly found herself hovering above a cold, foul smelling room filled with men in dirty clothes sleeping huddled on the bare floor with no blankets, sick, starved and barely alive. She was caught off guard as nothing like this had ever happened before. She was just starting to move around and really look at the men when just as suddenly she found herself once more sitting before her altar. She sat for a while trying to understand what had happened and then rose, put out the candle and checked the house for the night. In spite of her fatigue, she laid awake for a long time thinking about what she had seen and wondering if Colin had been one of the men. She fell asleep with tears in her eyes as she thought about Colin possibly being subjected to those wretched conditions.

Hannah and Sean arrived the next day with as many belongings as they had been able to bring. Hannah would be staying with Roberta and Tressa while Sean would stay in the restored building. Hannah told Roberta that they had planned to be married later in the year but had decided to have a simple ceremony as soon as possible, and they were married later that week at Francis' house with all of their friends present. After the wedding, the couple slept in the building that had been renovated, but they ate their meals with Roberta and Tressa.

Gasoline for the car was difficult to obtain, so they began using a horse and cart to travel to the rehab hospital to help with the wounded. Roberta had never had to sacrifice or do hard physical work, but she now found herself working harder than she had ever imagined possible. At times the pain and suffering of those they cared for became overwhelming for all of them, and Francis encouraged everyone to take some time off when they needed it no matter how much work was left to be done. One day when they had not received any new wounded for a while and many had recovered enough to leave, Francis and Roberta made a cup of tea and went to sit in a quiet corner by the fire to talk. They had barely spoken for weeks because of all the work that had to be done, so they were both glad to have this time together. They talked mostly about everyday things and then Roberta told Francis about the night she had been meditating and found herself in a strange place. She described the scene to Francis. They both agreed that she must have had an out of body experience and talked for a while about this and speculated about the possibility that she had actually traveled to where Colin was.

Chapter 22

It began to seem as though there would be no end to the war as month after month passed with a never-ending stream of mutilated bodies. Many of the young men who came to the rehab hospital had been told they would likely lose an arm or a leg but instead left intact. The rehab hospital was gaining a reputation for working miracles, but only a few people knew the secret to its success. Francis' patients in addition to being treated with modern medicine were provided with fresh, wholesome food and an atmosphere of balanced energy that allowed their bodies to heal much faster and more completely than they would have elsewhere. Every effort was made to prevent any discord from disturbing the balance. All of the large rooms on the lower level had been converted to wards with rows of cots. The small back parlor had been designated for new patients, and it was cleared and energized throughout the day to ensure the best results possible. As patients got stronger, they were moved to one of the larger rooms. There were some patients who didn't respond to the positive energy. These were given the best medical treatment possible and then sent to other hospitals to recover. Roberta always had her flute and lap harp with her and whenever there was a spare moment she and others played for the men. This not only brought comfort to patients but also served to help clear and balance the energy.

Even though she was very busy helping with the patients and the farm, she never once neglected the struggle to maintain the bond with Colin. Many nights she fell asleep sitting before her alter but never before the bond had been made and strengthened. For a long time, she hoped to return to that room she had visited while meditating in hopes of finding Colin, but as time passed she gave up.

As winter progressed, the weather made it difficult for Roberta, Hannah and Sean to travel to the rehab hospital, so they limited their visits to only once or twice a week; however, Hannah and Sean sometimes stayed for a few days at the rehab hospital if they were needed. There was a lot of time for Roberta and Hannah to work on their music and for Roberta to spend more time with Tressa. Roberta and Tressa grew very close on those long winter days alone, and Roberta discovered that her daughter had insight and wisdom far beyond her tender years. When asked how she knew things, Tressa said the bright ones told her things. Roberta began to notice that beings of light were often around Tressa.

Roberta had done little painting during the winter spending most of her time working on the music. Often as she sat gazing into the fire late at night, she was transported to a place where color and sound became one. She would reach for her flute and as she played music would see the colors of the notes swirl about the room. She often played the music that she wrote on those nights at the rehab hospital because it seemed to lift the spirits of the patients and ease their suffering.

Roberta awoke one day to find the sun shining warmly and decided to take a day off to paint. She packed her paints and a picnic lunch in the car, and she and Tressa headed for a hill that overlooked some ruins a few miles away. Tressa was three now and unusually quiet for a child, and Roberta wondered guiltily if she had neglected her too much. As they sat on the blanket eating their lunch and enjoying the sounds of nature, she drew her daughter into her arms and asked if she was lonely or unhappy. Tressa looked up and calmly answered that she was never lonely because her grandmother, grandfather and Aunt Diana were always around. Tressa said she couldn't understand how her aunt could be her age but it didn't matter because she liked playing with her. They talked for a while about how different things are after death and that there is no age on the other side. Roberta listened in stunned silence as Tressa talked about visiting strange places, described elementals that she played with and even told about riding on a flying unicorn. Tressa soon fell asleep and Roberta sat lost in thought and concern for her daughter as she began to paint the landscape before her. When Tressa awoke, she moved to set the painting aside and suddenly froze as she saw what she had painted. There were elementals under the trees, fairies flying through the air and even an angel in the clouds looking down on the scene below. She looked up from the painting and caught her breath as she saw the scene exactly as she had painted it. As a child, she had been told that these things were real and over the years had come to believe, but was still amazed by the wonder of it all.

Roberta wondered at times if she was endangering herself and her child by becoming so close to this world. This concern for her child grew until one day during meditation when her father appeared and told her that Tressa was in no danger but was, in fact, very blessed. Roberta was grateful for this reassurance when Tressa joined her one night while she was meditating. Roberta soon became aware that Tressa had connected to the bond between her and Colin and was also sending energy to her father. After that, Tressa often joined her mother in meditation. The next time that Roberta went to the rehab hospital, she took Tressa with her and watched as the child moved among the men seemingly oblivious to the horror or everything except their pain. As she moved among the men, she stopped occasionally to touch one of them gently and speak to them in a whisper.

After a few weeks, Roberta realized that most of the men Tressa spoke to died and became concerned once again. She brought the subject up casually one day and listened as Tressa explained how she was led to those who needed to be reassured about death so they wouldn't be so afraid. She said she explained to them that death was a chance to move away from pain and suffering to something beautiful. Roberta noticed that Tressa and Francis spent more and more time together. When asked, Francis told her he was able to share things with Tressa that he couldn't share with anyone else because of the gift they shared. As her own gift developed more rapidly with meditation, Roberta grew closer to both Francis and Tressa.

Chapter 23

In May, Francis and Megan were married in a simple ceremony at her family home and then returned to live in a small building away from the main house that Francis had remodeled to give them privacy. With better weather Roberta and Tressa spent more time at the rehab hospital. Roberta felt more and more lonely as she watched Francis and Megan together and saw their love grow deeper with each day. She still meditated and maintained the bond with Colin, but it seemed to grow weaker with each day. Her growing closeness with Tressa was the thing that kept her going when things seemed darkest during those days of war, death, and despair.

That summer was busier than ever. The rehab hospital was filled with wounded. Many people worked at the hospital caring for the patients but only a few worked with energy. Roberta often wanted to stay home and rest, but they were all needed to maintain the balanced energy necessary to help the patients heal. The only time that she stayed home was when she was needed to help at the farm with the food. Those who worked on the farm were very busy, and that year Francis had also hired people to farm his land in order to help provide enough food for the patients and people who worked at the rehab hospital.

Roberta arrived one day to find that a new group of wounded had come in. They were in very bad condition, and she hurried to the new arrival area to help work with the energy. As she worked, she suddenly realized that she had been so tired this morning she had overslept and forgotten to meditate. She worked for a while clearing and balancing the energy in the room, and then decided to take a few minutes to connect with Colin. As she made the connection, she was surprised to find that he seemed very close, and the bond was stronger. After a few minutes, she returned to the area where the new arrivals were to resume her work. She noticed Tressa with one of the men and felt sad at the thought that he was probably going to die. A short time later she glanced up to see that Tressa was still with the same man and decided to intervene out of concern for her daughter. As she approached the two, she saw her parents standing beside the bed and thought how strange it was that they were there. She glanced at the man on the bed as she reached for her daughter's hand to lead her away and everything suddenly went black.

Roberta awoke a few seconds later to find herself on the floor beside the bed and Francis worriedly asking what was wrong. She was struggling to sit up when her memory returned. She was unable to speak and tears flooded her eyes as she reached for the frail hand that lay on the covers. Francis was bewildered by her behavior until he took a closer look at the man in the bed and realized that this emaciated shell of a man was his brother-in-law Colin. He immediately gave orders to have an isolated alcove that looked out on the garden prepared and had Colin moved there.

They learned that the men were all from a prisoner of war camp that had been deserted by the Germans almost a week earlier. The men had been too weak to break out of the prison and would have died if not for some of the local people. They had been taken first to a hospital in France and then flown here since they were primarily Irish, and their condition was considered hopeless.

Roberta, Francis, and their friends from town spent the next few days making sure that the energy around Colin was kept balanced. Day after day, though Colin never responded, Roberta talked to him constantly as she cared for him. She insisted on doing everything for him herself and spent hours holding him upright as she fed him broth drop by drop. She bathed and shaved him, cut his hair, and changed his linens and clothes always talking quietly about the life they would have together when he was better. She slept next to him on the narrow bed with him cradled like a baby in her arms to share the warmth of her body as he seemed to always be cold. Megan, Francis and Tressa came and went, but no one made any attempt to persuade her to leave his side. The others helped care for Tressa, brought food for Roberta and helped to keep the energy balanced.

A few days after the men had arrived at the rehab hospital Roberta was singing softly as she bathed Colin when she looked up to see him watching her. He immediately closed his eyes again, and Roberta wondered if she had only imagined what happened. As Colin's body began to slowly regain strength, Roberta often sat beside him playing music. She was playing a piece that they had written together when she saw him open his eyes and look at her again. This time his eyes remained open for a while before slowly closing. From that time on his body regained strength rapidly, but he seemed unable to really communicate.

As soon as he was strong enough, Roberta insisted that Colin be moved to the cottage. He had only spoken a few words and seemed unsure where he was. Roberta was certain that the special energy of the cottage would help him to find his way back. She was encouraged when Colin uttered the word home as he was wheeled into the house and placed in the bed that had been set up in the main room beside the fireplace.

Tressa sat for hours talking softly to her father. Roberta never knew what she said, but he seemed to gain strength from these times. Francis phoned every day and stopped in at least twice a week to check on Colin. He was amazed at how rapidly he improved and admitted Roberta had been right about the cottage. Within a couple of weeks he was able to walk around the house by holding onto furniture and within a month he managed with Roberta's help to make his way outside to sit by the door in the sun.

Roberta called Colin's parents once he was home, and they came the following weekend to see him. She had considered calling them when he arrived at the rehab hospital, but she and Megan had discussed it and agreed to wait until he was better. They were very upset when Colin barely responded as they talked to him, and she was glad they had not seen him before his physical condition improved. Sean had to return to work but Kate stayed until the following weekend when Sean would be able to return for another visit. Roberta's heart went out to Kate as she tried day after day during that week to reach her son only to be met with a blank stare. The night before Sean and Kate were to return home, Colin finally recognized them, and the next day he was able to tell them goodbye when they left. They visited as often as possible after that and were encouraged by Colin's progress.

Roberta and Colin were sitting outside a couple of months after his move to the cottage when Colin finally began to talk in halting, clipped sentences. He said he had dreamed about her often and even thought he saw her once floating in the air above the room where he was imprisoned. In the next weeks, he told her there had been many times he wanted to give up and die but then he would feel her close and want to live to come home. He told her he had been captured after his plane was hit in a bombing run. Most of the men had died, but two of them had survived and had been tortured for weeks. As he talked about how he had suffered in the prison, Roberta told him how she had meditated to keep the bond strong and to send him energy, and she wondered now if she had been wrong. He reached for her hand and told her he was happy to be back home and grateful for the love that had brought him through that terrible ordeal. That night he joined her in their bedroom where they slept close together once again. Roberta was happy with the progress Colin was making, but she longed for more as she lay night after night next to the man she hardly knew anymore. Her happiness was complete when she awoke very early on a morning months later to find Colin caressing her gently and they made love finally as the sun rose on a chilly fall day. Roberta was grateful for the colder weather that kept them home more and gave them a chance to become reacquainted as Colin slowly found his way back.

The family gathered to spend Christmas with Sean and Kate again, and jokes were made about the romance of the blackout. But, even Sean's natural cheerfulness and efforts to lighten the mood failed to dispel the gloom. With sadness and extra long hugs everyone left early the day after Christmas in order to get back to their homes before dark as the blackout made night driving impossible. Colin was quiet during the visit and seemed relieved to be back in the peace and quiet of their little cottage with her and Tressa.

The news grew increasingly dismal during that winter, and everyone wondered if the whole world had gone mad. Roberta worried because Colin followed the news so closely on the radio, but he said he needed to know what was happening.

Chapter 24

By spring Colin was stronger and worked on the farm while Roberta returned to helping out at the rehab hospital. Colin still had times when he seemed to slip away and she was concerned when he said he wanted to go with her one day. She opened her mouth to protest but agreed when Tressa insisted they should all go together. It was a beautiful day, and Roberta and Tressa sang as they all rode in the cart. Colin asked why they didn't drive the car and seemed to become depressed when told that it was too difficult to get gasoline. It was wonderful to be out after being confined during the winter, and he seemed more cheerful by the time that they reached the hospital.

When they reached the rehab hospital, Roberta was surprised when Colin asked about the angels that were to be seen in every room. Colin became quite upset when he learned that the man he had been captured with had died. Everyone kept a close eye on him that day as he moved among the wounded, and Tressa stayed at his side. He spent a large part of the day with the men he had been imprisoned with. Roberta noticed that it seemed to help the men to talk to each other about things that they apparently weren't able to discuss with others, and she mentioned this to Francis. Colin was quiet on the way home, and Roberta worried that he was slipping away again. But, he seemed more like himself when they reached home and even had Tressa laughing when he played with her after dinner. That night when they went to bed, Roberta and Colin talked about the things Colin had seen at the rehab hospital. He seemed sad as he remarked that he was no longer frightened of the other world because it was so much better than the earthly one.

The next day while Roberta, Colin, and Tressa shared lunch with Megan and Francis, Francis asked Colin about an idea he had to see that the men had a time each day when they could talk among themselves without anyone else present. Colin agreed that this would be a good idea because it really helped him to be able to talk those who had shared the experience. Francis arranged for all the patients to be moved to the largest room each day where they were given a bell to ring if they needed help and left alone for up to two hours. For those patients who were unable to attend these gatherings, the other patients were encouraged to visit them whenever possible to include them in the discussions. Chairs and swings had also been placed throughout the grounds, and patients were taken outside and allowed to gather in groups to talk privately, but there was always staff available if needed.

That summer Colin stayed at the farm most of the time because he said he was more useful there. He improved even faster with physical activity, and his playful sense of humor returned. Roberta found herself making excuses to work at home to be close to Colin. One day when Roberta and Colin brought food to the hospital, Francis took her aside and told her to stay home and enjoy her happiness.

With the invasion of Normandy there were fewer patients coming to the rehab hospital and plenty of people to help, so Roberta was able to stay home without feeling guilty. Roberta and Colin worked hard on the farm, but they also took time off now and then to sneak away for a picnic. They talked for hours and worked together on music or Colin played music while Roberta painted. Colin saw more and more of the elemental world and accepted it now as a natural part of life. Roberta found him one day talking to a brilliant being of light and quietly returned to the house without disturbing them. When Colin returned to the cottage later that day, he seemed happier than he had been since before the war.

Christmas that year was wonderful with Colin's parents and everyone getting together at Francis and Megan's. The news from Europe was encouraging and everyone was hopeful of an end to the war soon. Francis and Megan were working on plans for a home close to the rehab hospital. Francis said that there would be many patients who would need a lot of care for years after the war was over, and he wanted to keep the rehab hospital for them. They all talked about their plans for the future, and Colin said he wasn't sure what he wanted to do yet. He and Roberta had talked about it, and he didn't want to return to the job he had done before the war. Their expenses at the cottage were low, and the farm brought in enough for them to live on, so there was no hurry to make a decision. Sean teased Colin about not wanting to leave Roberta long enough to go to work and laughed heartily as Colin agreed and Roberta blushed.

Roberta had always encouraged the people who worked on the farm to bring their children for Tressa to play with, and Tressa finally began to laugh and play like a normal child. She would be starting school soon, and Roberta was relieved to know that she enjoyed being with other children. Remembering her own experiences as a child, she did have one concern and mentioned to Tressa one day that she should be careful what she said because other people might not understand the special gift she had of seeing things they couldn't see. Tressa impatiently answered, as she ran off to play with her friends, that Grandmother Anne, Grandfather Robert and Uncle Francis had already explained that to her.

Spring came with a special gift that year as the war in Europe ended, and everyone felt renewed hope for the future. Roberta received letters from Mr. Hanson wanting to know when he could come over to do a recording and from Mr. Logan asking her to send paintings. She had done many paintings over the years, and she arranged to send them on the first ship going to The United States. Sean and Hannah still lived at the farm, and Roberta and Hannah had worked on the music a lot, so she wrote to Mr. Hanson telling him that she was ready whenever he could arrange it. She received a letter from Mr. Hanson a couple of weeks later saying that he had been unable to arrange a recording in Ireland because of the damage done by the war and asking if she would be able to come to his recording studio. Roberta was reluctant to leave Ireland but after discussing it with Colin, Tressa, Hannah and Sean, they decided to make the trip a vacation and go by ship since Colin was reluctant to fly. Colin and Tressa would join Hannah and Roberta for the recording since they had played the harp, lap harp and flute when Roberta and Hannah practiced and of course Hannah would sing. The arrangements were made to leave in a couple of weeks, and Roberta wrote informing Mr. Hanson of their arrival date. When Francis and Megan learned of the trip, they decided to join them on a delayed honeymoon.

Chapter 25

The group stood at the railing waving to Colin's family as the ship moved out to sea. They met each day on deck to practice until the captain suggested they practice in the lounge where everyone could listen to them in comfort. He refunded their money for the tickets and offered to pay them to entertain because the passengers liked them so much. This was welcome because Roberta and Colin had little money and had been relying on getting money from Mr. Logan for the paintings when they reached New York. They practiced twice a day and each time the lounge was packed to capacity.

Roberta had written to Mr. Logan to let him know when she would be arriving in New York, and they arrived early one morning to find a car waiting to take them to a hotel where Mr. Logan had booked a suite for them. The driver arranged for a cab to follow with the luggage and called ahead to arrange for rooms for Francis and Megan and Sean and Hannah.

It was good to be back on solid ground again, and after settling into the hotel they all met in the suite to make plans. Mr. Logan called to offer the car for the evening and invited them all to the gallery. He told Roberta that he had already sold a number of her paintings and had a sizeable check for her, and they arranged for the car to pick them up that afternoon. The women did a little shopping while the men went off on their own until time to leave for the gallery. Even though Roberta, Colin and Francis had been to New York before, it had changed a lot, so they were a little overwhelmed and grateful to have the car to get around the city.

Mr. Logan met them at the door and ushered them to a prominent place in the center of the gallery where Roberta's paintings had been hung. They had all seen her paintings before, but even Roberta was still amazed at the difference proper lighting made. Mr. Logan took Roberta and Colin to the office where he handed her a check, and they were both happily surprised when they saw the amount. Roberta explained that they would be leaving the following day and thanked Mr. Logan for everything as they left the gallery. The driver dropped them at a restaurant close to the hotel that Mr. Logan had suggested, and Colin told him they would walk back to the hotel. They gathered in the suite before retiring for the night to make plans for the next day.

The following morning after breakfast in the hotel dining room, Francis checked out while Colin and Roberta went to a bank down the street to cash the check and then returned to the hotel where three cabs were required to take them, their luggage and the musical instruments to the train station. After checking the luggage, they made their way to the observation car where they talked as they watched the scenery slide past. Tressa seemed to be enthralled with this country. It was fall, and the countryside was dazzling in a riot of color. While Ireland had a unique beauty of its own, Roberta had forgotten how beautiful her home country could be, and she felt a flood of conflicting feelings about being back here. After dinner in the dining car, they all returned to their compartments to rest until they reached their destination. Colin had arranged for the porter to wake him 30 minutes before arrival, and he woke the others while Roberta got herself and Tressa dressed. When they got off the train, Tressa voiced her relief that this town wasn't like New York, and they all laughed and admitted to feeling the same way.

It was very late when they finally got checked into the hotel, and they said goodnight grateful to retire to their rooms for a good night's sleep. They had arrived a day earlier than expected and took advantage of that to explore the town and relax before Roberta called Mr. Hanson in the afternoon. Arrangements were made to meet the following morning to go over the music and make the final selection and then begin recording the next day. Roberta sensed that Colin needed some quiet time and suggested the others take in a movie after dinner. Francis understood and offered to take Tressa with them. Roberta and Colin walked to a park close to the hotel where they sat in silence letting the stillness of the evening bring peace to Colin and then they talked quietly for a while before returning to the hotel to fall asleep in each other's arms. Francis and Megan kept Tressa with them that night, but she rushed in early the next morning chattering about the movie.

Francis and Megan stayed in the dining room the next morning after Roberta, Colin, Tressa, Hannah and Sean ate a hasty breakfast and then left for the recording studio. They played the music that they had brought with them, and it took most of the day to agree on what to use. Mr. Hanson tried to talk them into recording more, but Roberta remained firm. The four of them spent the rest of the day practicing to get everything arranged so that they could begin recording the next morning. They arrived at the hotel to find that Francis and Megan had decided to do some touring on their own. They had rented a car and left a message they would be back in two days.

Roberta, Hannah, Tressa, and Colin had played together so much that the recording went well and was finished by the time that Francis and Megan returned to town. Roberta had even agreed to recording an additional single of one piece of music that she and Colin had written before the war with another of her favorites on the other side.

They had booked return passage for the following week, so after discussing what to do for the remaining time, it was decided that they would go to the beach for a few days before returning to New York. Roberta and Francis were the only ones who had ever seen a real beach before, and the ocean entranced even them. It seemed cold to the people who lived there, but the group from Ireland welcomed the relief from the unaccustomed heat.

They arrived in New York and boarded the ship the night before it sailed without having to stay in the city. The others went inside while Francis and Roberta stood at the rail watching as their native land slipped away with their feelings in turmoil. It no longer felt like home and yet they felt a deep longing to hold onto it. They talked about these feelings and the fact that they no longer really belonged anywhere. They turned to go inside and saw the faint image of all those they had loved standing on the deck and understood that home is wherever you make it.

Chapter 26

As the ship drew near the coast of Ireland, Roberta felt the familiar sense of coming home and knew that she truly did belong to this mystical land. She glanced at Francis and they both smiled at the certain knowledge that this was indeed home. Francis and Megan had broken the news that they were going to have a baby the day before. They had wanted to tell Megan's parents first but were just too excited to keep the news to themselves, so everyone was sworn to secrecy until they had a chance to tell Sean and Kate who were to visit that weekend.

Tressa started school a week after they returned from their trip, and Roberta and Colin had time each day alone. Colin seemed to slip away a lot, and Roberta wondered if the trip had been too soon for him. They talked about this, and Colin admitted that he had been afraid at first but he felt it had been good for him to be forced to go out among people. That winter they took long walks and worked on music together. Roberta saw the healing as Colin gradually began to take more interest in what was going on around him. They often visited Francis and Megan and Colin always spent some time with the patients, which seemed to benefit him as much as those he visited.

At Christmas, the family all gathered at Sean and Kate's for the first truly festive Christmas they had enjoyed for a long time. Claire had married the year before and she and her husband Daniel joined them. After Christmas dinner, Roberta announced that she and Colin had a gift of their own because they were to have another baby. She laughed as Sean swung her around joking that he must not want the baby to be born because he was trying to squeeze it out of her while Kate fussed at him to put her down before he hurt her or the baby. They all stayed with Sean and Kate until after the New Year and left with smiles and plans to see each other soon.

Life settled into a routine of school for Tressa, work at the rehab hospital or on the farm for Roberta and Colin and church on Sunday with their friends. Colin yelled at Roberta one day when she tried to tell him how he should do something. They both stood frozen for a moment and then fell into each other's arms laughing as she remarked that he was obviously back to his old self. She had been so used to doing everything and making all the decisions for so long that it had become a habit. After that, Colin's confidence returned as she relied on him more, and she was relieved to have someone to share the responsibilities and decision-making.

With the new baby coming, a decision had to be made about living quarters. This led to another argument as Roberta steadfastly refused to move from the cottage. Of course other arguments arose when they tried to decide how to add onto the cottage to provide enough room for all of them. Colin insisted on adding onto the side but Roberta wanted to add a second story to better preserve the original cottage. This time it almost got out of hand before Roberta remembered the argument early in their marriage and suddenly stopped in mid sentence. They agreed to ask for help and drove over to ask Francis and Megan for their opinion. After they had explained what they wanted to do and discussed the options, Francis and Megan agreed with Roberta that a second story would better preserve the character of the cottage and be easier to heat even though it would be more difficult to build because of having to take the roof off the house. Francis and Colin discussed the building while Roberta and Megan talked about their pregnancies and other things related to the home. By the time the weather was warm and dry enough to begin work on the cottage, plans had been worked out and materials ordered. The work began on a bright, sunny day in May and by the end of the week the second story was closed in.

Megan and Francis' son Patrick had been born the end of March. Sean and Kate had visited for a week, and it was like a holiday for everyone. Roberta was in her seventh month and much larger than she had been with Tressa when Sean and Kate came for another visit and Kate remarked that there were twins on her side of the family. A few weeks later, Francis examined Roberta and said he was sure he had heard two heartbeats. He teased her about having to do better than anyone else as he kissed her on the cheek and assured her he would be there when the time came for her to deliver.

Roberta awoke one night the end of June with pain shooting from her back into her stomach. It lasted for a short while and then stopped only to wake her again about 20 minutes later. After the pain stopped she eased out of bed to avoid waking Colin and went downstairs where she built a fire and made a cup of tea. By the time that Tressa was ready for school and breakfast prepared, the pains were 10 minutes apart, and she called Francis. She managed to hide the fact that she was in labor until after Tressa left for school. Francis arrived shortly after Tressa left and examined Roberta. He reassured them that everything was normal and sent Colin to bring Hannah and Rose to help Roberta. While the women helped Roberta change and got everything ready, Francis took Colin outside to calm him down. By noon Roberta's pains were very close together and much sooner than Francis had expected the first baby was born followed almost immediately by the second. The women cleaned and cared for the babies while Francis took care of Roberta and then called Colin to come in and see his sons. The boys were small but fully developed and seemingly healthy. Though the birth had been relatively easy, Roberta was exhausted and fell into a deep sleep after a quick look at her sons.

Roberta awoke to the sound of the babies crying and had Colin bring them to be fed. Tressa was home from school and watched in fascination as the little mouths greedily sucked. In the following weeks, Roberta was glad to have Colin, Rose and Hannah to call on as the babies demanded constant attention. When one began to cry the other joined in, and there were times when she wanted to cry with them.

The boys had been named Blair Sean and Carlin Robert after both their grandfathers. When Sean and Kate came to see their new grandsons, Roberta realized how much she missed her parents and wished they could be with her now. A short time later, her parents appeared and kissed each of the twins before fading away and once again she was reminded how lucky she was to be able to have them with her even though they were gone.

Chapter 27

Tressa was telling Roberta about something that had happened at school one day when first one and then both twins began to cry. She threw her books on the floor and ran outside yelling that she wished they would go away. As Roberta went to get the boys, she realized that she sometimes felt the same way and instantly said a prayer asking for forgiveness. As soon as the twins had been fed and changed, Roberta asked Rose to keep an eye on them and went in search of her daughter. She found Tressa sitting on the bank of a stream a mile from the house. She put her arm around Tressa pulled her head into her lap and sat stroking the auburn hair. When Tressa had been young, there had been only Tressa and Roberta, and she realized that she had not spent any time alone with her daughter for a long time. She talked about the days when they had been alone and how lucky they were to have had that time and now to have so many people in their family. She also admitted there were times when she was tired that she wished the boys were gone, but she said she didn't really mean it and would be very unhappy if anything happened to them. Tressa told her about her day at school while they walked back to the house. The next day Roberta arranged for Rose to watch the boys for a while each day when Tressa got home from school so that she could have time with her uninterrupted.

The twins grew rapidly and were soon into everything. They were very inquisitive and had to be watched every minute to keep them from harm, and Roberta found herself longing for the time when they would be old enough to go to school. She had never had to discipline Tressa. The boys, however, were totally different. They were three years old the day she caught them trying to drive the car and realized something had to be done as they had been told twice before about this. Without a word, she went to the house, returned with one of their father's belts and proceeded to spank them soundly on their bottoms. They remained very energetic and inquisitive, but from that time on they listened and were much easier to handle. Though Colin teased Roberta about being a tyrant, he was relieved that she had taken care of that because he adored his sons and found it very difficult to be firm with them about anything.

The farm was very successful and Colin was needed to oversee everything, so he had stopped talking about needing to look for a job. For her part, Roberta was happy to know that he was always there and she could talk to him whenever she wanted. The recording they had made was still bringing in money, and Mr. Logan had written several times to send checks and ask for more paintings, so they had more than enough money.

When the boys started school, Roberta and Colin enjoyed their new freedom alone with each other and often disappeared during the day on a picnic or a long walk. These were healing times for both of them after all that they had been through, and they grew even closer as they were finally able to talk about the war years. Roberta had time to paint again, and she and Colin played and wrote music during these quiet times while the children were at school.

Claire and her husband had moved to England, and thereafter holidays were always celebrated at Francis and Megan's as they had a large house, and it was easier for Kate and Sean to visit than it was to take all of the children to them. Francis and Megan had a daughter named Maureen the year after the twins were born and another they named Helena two years later. Francis and Megan weren't good at discipline and when the six children were together bedlam prevailed, until Roberta finally stepped in one day and took control of the situation with her belt. After that, everyone jokingly referred her to as the tyrant. However, the children never doubted that she loved them, and the adults were relieved to have sanity restored.

The two families went through the childhood diseases together because they spent so much time together that what one child got the others were certain to share. The boys were always into something and Maureen usually joined them, but Helena was more like Tressa, and they spent a great deal of their time together.

Francis kept the rehab hospital open as a long-term care facility for veterans and turned part of the downstairs into a clinic for an ever-growing private practice. Roberta and Colin often visited and played music for the patients to help keep the energy balanced. It was after one of these visits that Colin mentioned having seen the spirits of soldiers wandering in the house and grounds. Roberta had not seen them, but the following day they returned to talk to Francis about this. They met at the rehab hospital late that night and found that many spirits had become trapped there over the years. Once again, Francis called on their friends from town and with their help after several sessions all of the spirits had been helped to cross over to the light and find peace.

The years passed in happiness enlivened by the antics of the children with the two families so close as to be almost one. When Sean retired, Francis, Megan, Colin and Roberta bought a small place between their two homes for Sean and Kate. They had talked about selling the family home but it had been in the family for many generations and the children didn't want to see it sold. They all hoped that one of the grandchildren might someday want to live there and carry on the tradition.

All of the children spent a lot of time with Sean and Kate. Though they loved all of the children Kate was closer to Tressa and Helena while Sean preferred the others because they were more energetic. As the children grew older, the parents often joked that they longed for the days when all they had to worry about was the war. It seemed that the boys and Maureen were always in trouble at school mostly because they were too energetic and disrupted the class. The twins had told Roberta and Colin that their teacher was a bully and just didn't like them, but Roberta always disciplined the boys whenever they got into trouble.

The twins came home one day from school with bleeding stripes on their backs. When asked what had happened they said they had laughed at something the teacher said, and he had beaten them in front of the class. The boys stayed home the next day while Roberta and Colin went to speak with the teacher. The teacher would not tell them what had happened the day before but simply said the boys were always a problem and had to be straightened out. When Roberta asked again what they had done, he became angry and said they were just devil worshipers and needed to have the devil whipped out of them and refused to say anything more.

When they reached home, Roberta and Colin asked what the teacher had meant and were told that he had overhead the children talking about the spirits at the rehab hospital and the elementals. After that he had talked about them being evil. That night Roberta and Colin took the children to visit Megan and Francis to talk about what had happened. As they questioned the children, they were all shocked to learn how all of the children had been belittled and ridiculed by several of the teachers. The next day the children were enrolled in a private school, and a letter was sent to the school complaining about the teachers. Roberta blamed herself for not having foreseen this after what had happened to her, but the boys had never seemed to notice and Tressa had been warned. They learned a few years later that two of the teachers in question were fired because there had been so many complaints about them.

The children were more careful about discussing the things that were taken for granted at home and did very well at the new school. The boys excelled at sports, and Maureen was active in plays and social activities. Tressa and Helena were interested in art and music and joined the orchestra. Though the children were loved and spoiled to a certain extent, they all had chores and worked with their parents on the farm and in the rehab hospital and helped their grandparents.

Chapter 28

Tressa surprised everyone when asked what she wanted for her sixteenth birthday by saying she wanted to visit the United States during summer vacation. Roberta's first impulse was to refuse, but she remembered how important her trip to Ireland had been to her and agreed. Mr. Hanson had contacted them several times about doing another record, so Roberta and Colin decided to go with Tressa and record another album. They also asked Francis and Megan to let Helena go with them on the trip and play for the recording.

Excitement mounted as the end of the school year approached. Roberta had sorted through all of the paintings and she and Colin packed those to send to New York. They all spent hours pouring over books and maps planning their itinerary. Roberta notified Mr. Logan at the gallery and Mr. Hanson that they would be coming to New York and arranged a date three days after their arrival in New York to meet with Mr. Hanson. After the recording was finished, they planned to rent a car and drive across the country for a month or so to the places they had marked on the map until they were ready to return home.

Once again, they practiced on the ship and were even paid a small amount to entertain the other passengers. Mr. Logan had arranged for hotel rooms and had a car waiting for them. He contacted Roberta the morning after they arrived to arrange a visit to the gallery and to let her know that the paintings had arrived a couple of weeks earlier and many had already been sold. When they arrived at the gallery, Mr. Logan told them that he had requests for Roberta's work all the time. He then asked her how she would feel about selling prints of her work. He explained that since prints would be less expensive more people could enjoy her work. Roberta had often regretted that only the wealthy could enjoy her work and the idea of being able to share her gift with more people made her very happy, so she readily agreed.

They had checked out of the hotel before going to the gallery and after cashing the check Mr. Hanson had given Roberta, they had the car take them to the railway station. Even though they would be on the train all night, they were all eager to be out of the city and on their way as soon as possible. The trip was hot and dusty, and most of the clothing they had was much too warm for this climate, so the first day was spent shopping and sightseeing.

The next day they arrived at the studio with music and instruments to begin the task of selecting music to record. One of the pieces that Roberta had written late at night while Colin was missing had inadvertently been included, and Mr. Hanson asked them to play it. When they finished, he was obviously shaken and said that piece definitely had to be included. By the end of that day, the pieces to be recorded had been selected, and they arranged to meet early the next morning to begin recording. Mr. Hanson asked them to record the special piece first. He opened the speakers to the entire building as they played the piece, and everyone in the studio stopped what they were doing to listen. They recorded two other pieces that day, and when they left everyone in the building stood and clapped. The recording was finished in five days. They had more music and Mr. Hanson urged them to do another recording before they left, but Colin was showing signs of stress and Roberta refused to record anymore.

Roberta had kept in touch with Judy over the years and asked if anyone would mind taking time to stop for a quick visit. Of course, everyone agreed, and they took a bus to the nearby town where Judy lived the next morning. Judy and Roberta sat up late into the night catching up on all the news and talking about growing up at the clinic and the people they had loved. Judy told Roberta that she had gone to the clinic a few years back but didn't stop because it was different, and Roberta told her about the time that she and Francis had driven out for a visit only to leave without stopping. Judy began to cry when Roberta asked about Hank and said he had been killed a few months earlier while robbing a store. Roberta held Judy as she cried and explained that Hank had never been able to overcome the abuse he had suffered as a child.

The following morning, they talked over their plans as they sipped coffee, and Judy suggested they ride busses wherever they wanted to go rather than bother with a car. They all agreed this was a better idea because Colin could enjoy the trip more without worrying about breakdowns along the way. Judy drove them to the bus station where they looked over bus schedules and adjusted their itinerary while they waited for the bus that would take them on the first leg of their journey. As the bus pulled away, Roberta leaned out the window waving until she could no longer see Judy standing on the curb. The visit had brought up many forgotten memories, and she was lost in thought most of the day not even noticing the countryside until they reached the mountains. The girls were so excited they constantly switched seats in order to see everything. They ate lunch that day at an outdoor café on the side of a hill and hated to leave because it was so beautiful and so much cooler.

The journey westward across the upper United States with stops at spots of interest along the way was enjoyable and they reached San Francisco a week later. They stayed in San Francisco for three days during which time they took a taxi across the Golden Gate Bridge, visited Chinatown, rode the trolley cars, and ate at Fisherman's Wharf. Very early on the fourth morning they boarded a bus south to begin the return journey across the lower United States. They stayed for a day in Santa Barbara enjoying the unique beauty of the architecture and then boarded a bus to Arizona where they visited the Grand Canyon and the Painted Desert.

Despite the heat, Roberta and Tressa were captivated by the mysterious quality of the desert. They stayed two days in Arizona near the Painted Desert while Roberta and the girls tried to capture the essence of the desert in sketches and chalk and Colin took many color photographs. They slowly made their way across Arizona and New Mexico stopping at towns throughout the desert talking to the people and marveling at the similarities in their beliefs and many of the people in this area, especially the American Indians.

The landscape slowly changed as the bus moved across Texas and then into Louisiana. In New Orleans they took a boat up the Mississippi River and toured two of the River Plantations before returning to stay overnight at a hotel in the French Quarter. In spite of the clothing they had bought, they all found the heat here to be unbearable. They were up very early the next morning and after a quick tour of the French Quarter once again boarded a bus to continue east along the gulf coast.

As the bus moved across the country, the four of them talked about the things they had seen and the feelings evoked by them. Roberta and Colin were often amused and just as often astounded as they listened to the girls talk about their innermost feelings. They began to see the girls not only as their daughter and niece but also as young people with their futures ahead of them with unlimited possibilities.

They spent a few days at a small town in Alabama where they enjoyed the welcome relief from the heat offered by the ocean. Roberta and Colin wandered the beach late one night after the girls were in bed and made love under the stars. They girls had led very sheltered lives, and they enjoyed the attention they received from many young men on the beach. Roberta and Colin stayed close by and remained watchful while they allowed the girls as much freedom as safely possible. When they boarded the bus once again to continue their journey, Roberta and Colin were relieved while the girls wished they could stay longer.

Their original plan had been to continue east until they reached the east coast, but in hopes of avoiding some of the heat, they had decided to travel north through the mountains of Tennessee, Kentucky, and Virginia instead. The scenery was beautiful, and they stopped often to stay overnight in a small town to get a shower and a good night's sleep before continuing their trip. In the sparsely populated area deep in the mountains where there were few jobs, they were struck by the stark contrast of the beauty of the landscape and the ugly poverty and hopelessness of the people. The plight of these people was so great and they wondered how such a rich country could allow this to exist. They all felt guilty relief when the road once again led to more prosperous areas, but the faces of those people, especially the children, stayed with them for the rest of their lives.

The remainder of the trip was enjoyable with stops to visit Washington DC and historical sites along the way. They reached New York the day before the ship sailed and visited the gallery where once again Mr. Logan gave Roberta a check. Mr. Logan told them that the idea of selling prints of her work was proving to be very successful. Roberta talked about the things they had seen on the trip and ideas she had for paintings, and he assured her that he would be happy to handle anything she sent.

They bought some art supplies before boarding the ship, and Roberta and the girls spent most of their days on deck painting the things they had seen while Colin sat nearby or wandered the decks talking to the other passengers. Helena did many paintings of the people of the Appalachian Mountains, and Roberta marveled at the depth of these. Most of Tressa's paintings were of the desert while Roberta worked on both. As they worked, many people showed interest and they each managed to sell a few pieces. The second day on board Colin met an American who had fought in the war and been stationed in Ireland. They spent a lot of their time together sharing their experiences, and Roberta was relieved to be able to paint without worrying about neglecting him. They all spent their evenings on deck and often played music softly as they were humbled by the vastness of the ocean and the star-studded sky overhead. There was a meteor shower on the third night out and they joked about how God had arranged such wonderful fireworks just for them.

Chapter 29

Francis and Megan were waiting when the ship docked very early on a foggy, chilly morning. The ride home was noisy as both girls talked at once about the things they had seen and Francis and Megan tried to understand what they were saying. Roberta and Colin were happy to be home once again where it was cooler. They had the pictures from the trip processed, and Roberta spent hours painting to capture the ever-changing colors and mystical quality of the desert as well as the beauty of the mountains and the contrasting poverty and despair of the people who lived there.

Colin and Megan's father Sean died suddenly of a heart attack just over a month after they returned from their trip. Both families traveled back to the family home to have him laid to rest with the other family members, and Claire returned from England for the funeral. Roberta became concerned as Colin once again retreated into himself, but he returned from a walk the night after the funeral to tell her that everything was all right because he had met and talked with his father. As they stood outside the house saying their goodbyes before returning home, Roberta looked up to see Sean standing at the drawing room window and turned to see Colin wave goodbye to his father as he got into the car.

Megan and Francis tried to get Kate to come live with them, but she refused saying she wanted to have her own home. Tressa and/or Helena stayed overnight with her, and of course the other family members visited as often as possible to keep her from being too lonely. Roberta arrived one day to find Kate in high spirits. Kate excitedly led her into the kitchen where she put on the kettle to make tea and then told her that Sean had visited her that morning after Helena left for school. Tears poured down her cheeks as she talked about how young and healthy he had looked. She said he had talked to her about death and how it wasn't at all what we were told but merely a shift in reality and release of the physical restrictions. The two women talked for hours as Roberta told her about the things they had been told by family members who had passed through the veil from this life. An even closer bond was formed between them that day that was never broken.

From that time on, Kate embraced life with renewed purpose. She asked Roberta to teach her to drive in secret and then surprised everyone by showing up at church one Sunday driving her own car. From that time, she volunteered at the rehab hospital and at church functions. She often spent a day alone with Colin, which helped both of them cope with their loss.

Roberta was busy caring for the house and her family, but she had time each day to devote to painting or music and she and Colin played and wrote music at night by the fire. From their births the children had almost always fallen asleep to the sound of music that took them into magical worlds in their dreams. Blair and Carlan had complained about not being able to go to sleep while their parents were away on the trip because of not having music, and Hannah had played for them each night.

The boys remained mischievous and energetic and Roberta often felt exhausted by them. She had never felt as close to them as she did to Tressa and felt guilty about not loving them as much. It was a chilly day in May with a light rain that she realized she loved them more than she had suspected. Blair came running in the house shortly after they had returned from school yelling that Carlan was hurt. Roberta ran after him to find Carlan lying unconscious on the ground. As she checked to be certain that he was breathing, love for this beautiful child welled up in her chest. She checked for broken bones or injuries, while Blair explained that they had climbed the large tree with long ropes and had planned to tie them around their waists and frighten Tressa by suddenly jumping out of the tree when she came by. Carlan had been leaning to tie the rope around a large branch when he lost his footing and fell. Roberta used her healing skills and couldn't detect any injuries, but she was afraid to move him. She sent Blair to call Francis, folded her apron and carefully placed it under his head as a pillow. As she sat beside Carlan trying to shelter him from the rain, it was as though she were really seeing him for the first time. The twins were so much like Colin had been when she first met him that she suddenly felt almost overwhelming love for them. Blair returned to tell her that Uncle Francis was coming right over. He looked so lonely sitting there obviously worrying about his brother and feeling guilty that Roberta forgot about being angry. She reached to take him in her arms, and he broke down with great wrenching sobs. They both jumped when Carlan suddenly began laughing and Blair quickly pulled away and wiped his tears. Roberta made Carlan stay where he was until Francis arrived and confirmed that he seemed to be fine. Roberta took both boys in her arms and kissed them against their protests and then proceeded to give them a thorough tongue-lashing. Francis smiled as he watched the two boys squirm under her anger and almost felt sorry for them.

The boys finally managed, with great relief, to escape and Francis returned to the house with Roberta for a cup of tea. They seldom had time alone anymore, and it was good to just sit and talk without anyone else around. He asked about how Colin was handling the death of his father, and then about Kate and was glad that they both had been able to see Sean. Roberta told him about the visit with Judy when they had been in the United States and about Hank. She had not wanted to mention this in front of others because Francis had been so close to Hank. When Francis wondered aloud if he might have been able to help if he had made more of an effort to stay close to Hank, Roberta pointed out that his own sister had been unable to help him. They talked for a while about everyday things and then lingered in a close embrace as Francis was leaving both glad to have had this special time together.

Colin had gone to visit his mother that day and when he returned, Roberta told him what had happened with the boys. As she talked, she saw fear in his eyes and hurriedly assured him that Francis had checked Carlan thoroughly and was certain he was unhurt. He called the boys and then shocked them all when he proceeded to take the belt to both of them. The boys were more affected by the fact that it was their adoring father who disciplined them than by the discipline itself and were subdued for days. This day marked a change in the relationship of the boys to both their parents with them feeling closer to their mother and having more respect as well as love for their father. They still continued to get into mischief, but they never again did something that was so dangerous.

Tressa and Helena remained very close and spent most of their time together. Roberta missed the closeness she had with Tressa, but she was happy that she had someone close to her age to share things with. The girls often talked about the trip they had all taken and Roberta felt uneasy as she listened to them talk. It was no surprise to Roberta when Tressa announced in her senior year that she wanted to go to college in Arizona. Colin immediately said no, and her first instinct was to agree, but she remembered the way she had felt when she was there and understood. It took both of them to finally convince Colin that she had to make her own decisions. Roberta pointed out that they could record more music and visit Tressa often.

Tressa left for college the next fall, and Roberta felt lost. She found herself unable to settle down to anything. She visited Kate one day and talked to her about what she was experiencing and was surprised to learn that Kate had cried for weeks whenever a child had left home even though they had all been close by until Claire had moved to England. She admitted that moving so close to Megan and Colin had been more of a blessing for her than anyone, even Sean, had known.

With Tressa gone, Roberta spent more time with Kate and she remarked to Colin one day that she felt like Kate should not live alone anymore. When Sean died, Kate had confided in Roberta that she couldn't stay with Francis and Megan because their children were so unruly. Roberta had offered then to have her live with them and told Colin that she would love to have Kate with them. With Tressa gone, they had an extra room, and it would be quieter than at Francis and Megan's. Roberta visited Francis the next day and managed to get him alone to discuss this before approaching Megan. The house was chaos with the children running and screaming and Roberta understood why Kate couldn't stand that. Francis said he would talk to Megan that night but was sure she wouldn't mind as she had her hands full with the children.

Megan called the next day to let Roberta know that she wouldn't be offended if her mother wanted to live with Roberta and Colin, and Roberta and Colin went over that afternoon to talk to Kate. They explained that it would really be easier on all of them if she lived at the cottage, and she finally agreed. They had fewer people working at the farm than during the war, so they decided to surprise Kate by combining and fixing the two rooms that had been used for workers to allow her to have her own space. Hannah and Sean lived in the other half, so she could call on them in an emergency. Kate had been resigned to living in the house with them but was very happy when she saw what they had done. A few weeks later, she admitted that she was really much happier there than she had been alone, but she continued to do her volunteer work and stay busy.

Chapter 30

Tressa wrote often obviously very happy and excited about her life. She had gotten a job working with the Indian children on the reservation in her spare time. She was always vague when questioned about her studies and just mentioned classes she was taking. They had expected her to come home for the holidays and were very disappointed when she said that she needed to do some work for extra credit and wouldn't be able to make it. They talked about going over to record some music but decided to wait until the next year. It seemed like a lifetime before summer arrived and Tressa finally told them when she would be home. Roberta couldn't sleep the night before from excitement, and they arrived at the airport in Dublin more than an hour early.

When Tressa stepped off the plane, Roberta was struck by the sudden realization that her little girl was gone forever replaced by a lovely, confident young woman. On the drive home Tressa talked some about college but mostly her work on the reservation and how much she was learning about the people and how spiritual they were. She didn't mention any boyfriends and when asked was very noncommittal. When they reached the cottage, all the family and many friends were at the house, and tables laden with food had been set up in the yard for a welcome home party.

The following morning Tressa was up early and helped Roberta with breakfast. After breakfast, Colin and the boys went to work on the farm, and Roberta and Tressa were alone for the first time. They talked as they did the housework about the family and Tressa talked about her life at school. When the work was finished, they got a cup of tea and went to sit outside before lunch. Roberta suddenly sensed that there was something

Tressa wanted to tell her and felt a growing sense of dread. Tressa finally said that she had switched from a four-year degree curriculum to nursing and planned to move to the reservation where she could help the Indians. She talked about the deep spirituality of the people and how so many were losing this and turning to alcohol and lives of aimlessness. She then took Roberta's hand and looked her in the eye as she said she had met a young Indian man and they planned to be married when she returned. Roberta wasn't sure what she had expected but it had certainly not been this, and she sat stunned as Tressa talked about the life she would have and how much she could help these people. As she talked about had strongly she was drawn to the desert and the people, Roberta remembered her own feelings of reverence and peace when they had visited. Although the pain of knowing that her only daughter would be so far away was intense, she understood why Tressa felt the way she did and was happy that she had found someone to share her life.

That night, Roberta and Tressa told Colin what Tressa's plans were and sat quietly while he ranted and raved about how he wouldn't allow her to throw her life away like this. After about 10 minutes of this, Tressa walked over, put her arms around his neck and kissed him on the cheek. He sat quietly fuming for about a minute and then surprised them both by saying it looked like he was going to have to get over his fear of flying or spend the rest of his life on the ocean going back and forth between Ireland and the United States. The one thing that he absolutely insisted on was that he be there to give the bride away. They all agreed that because of the heat it would be better to wait and have the wedding in the early fall. They broke the news to the rest of the family that weekend. Roberta was surprised that Helena wasn't more upset and then realized that she had probably known all along. She also wondered if Francis and Megan might be in for their own surprise as Helena and Tressa spent a lot of time together whispering. Both Tressa and Helena begged until Francis and Megan finally agreed to allow Helena to make the trip with Roberta and Colin to be a part of the wedding.

Tressa stayed for three weeks but it seemed like only days to Roberta when she and Colin took her to the airport. On the way home, Roberta sat with Colin's arm around her shoulder lost in memories of those years when she and Tressa had only had each other. There had been many turns in the road that led them to this day, and as she let her mind wander through the years she said a silent prayer for the many blessings she had received.

Roberta contacted Mr. Hanson to let him know that she would be in the States in October and they arranged for a recording session after the wedding. She had sent paintings to Mr. Logan earlier and received a large check just in time to help with the expenses of the trip. The prints had been selling extremely well, and money was less of an issue that it had been in the past, but it was good to have some extra money in case of an emergency. Tressa had suggested they arrive before the wedding so that they could get to know the people who would be her new family. She also wanted some extra time for shopping because she wanted to share that with Roberta.

Roberta knew that Colin was very nervous about flying again and suggested that they go by ship to New York and then fly to Arizona in order to let him become accustomed to flying over land rather than the long flight over the ocean. Colin seemed quite relieved and even became excited about the trip. Blair, Carlan and Helena would also be going. The boys were quite talented with the guitar and lap harp and were excited about the prospect of being included in the recording sessions with Helena, Roberta and Colin. The trip over would give them all time to practice together and be ready when the time came to record.

A new lap harp and flute were bought in order for them to have enough instruments as well as clothing for the warmer climate. As the time to leave drew close, Roberta packed and repacked suitcases and double-checked every detail. The boys were excited about the trip and were even more rowdy than usual, so by the time they were to leave, Roberta's nerves were thoroughly frayed. The entire family accompanied them to the dock and stood waving as the ship moved out to sea. Colin had to take the boys to task almost immediately to stop them from running all over the ship, and Roberta settled in a deck chair to relax relieved to have him handle this.

The next morning they gathered on deck to practice and were invited by the Captain to use the main area so that other passengers could sit and listen. Each morning and afternoon they practiced for a few hours and the rest of the day was their own to do as they wished. Of course, limits had to be placed on the boys and Helena, so Roberta and Colin didn't get to relax as much as they would have liked. Roberta spent most of her days worrying that the boys were going to fall overboard.

They had rough seas from a storm for two days, but because Francis had given them medicine they all avoided the seasickness that plagued most of the other passengers. The crossing was otherwise without incident, and the ship docked early on a beautiful fall day. It was a relief to be back on land and they laughed and teased each other as they staggered when trying to walk on land after being used to the rolling of the deck on the ship.

Their plane didn't leave until the next afternoon, so after checking into a hotel they visited the Empire State Building and Statue of Liberty. Blair and Carlan had never seen a city other than Dublin and were for once subdued by the sheer size and bustle of the city. They were all tired and slept soundly that night in spite of the noise of the city. Roberta shared a room with Helena and Colin shared a room with the boys. It was barely daylight when the boys burst into Roberta and Helen's room early the next morning eager to be out, and Roberta groaned as she left the luxury of the bed. After breakfast, they did some shopping and sightseeing until lunch and then returned to the hotel to pack and leave for the airport.

Chapter 31

As the plane lifted into the air, Colin's hands trembled and Roberta spoke soft words of encouragement as she held both of his hands in hers until he finally relaxed. The flight was very smooth and the scenery was beautiful with the trees in full fall color. They made one stop to refuel, and Colin seemed more relaxed during takeoff than before. He was, however, obviously relieved when the plane landed in Arizona and gave Roberta a quick kiss as they stood to leave the plane. Helena and the boys had enjoyed the flight and were bubbling over with excitement. As they stepped from the plane, the heat hit them and Roberta was very glad that Tressa had agreed to wait until fall to have her wedding.

Tressa rushed to meet them wearing a light cotton dress with her hair pulled back in a ponytail. She quickly introduced them to the young man waiting with her as her fiancé John Running Deer. He shook hands with Colin and then turned to Roberta. As she looked into his eyes, she knew that everything was exactly the way it should be and surprised him by kissing him on the cheek and giving him a hug. The men retrieved the luggage and musical instruments, and they all piled into the pickup with Colin, Helena and the boys in the back. Though it only took an hour, the ride was hot and dusty and seemed much longer as they bounced over rough roads. Arrangements had been made for them at a hotel close to the reservation, and the coolness of the lobby was a relief to them all.

They had a light lunch in the hotel dinning room and talked about the trip and general plans for the wedding. Tressa suggested that they rest during the heat of the day and she and John would return to take them to the reservation around six o'clock that evening. She had brought a couple of light cotton dresses for Helena and Roberta and light slacks and loose fitting shirts for Colin and the twins. After Tressa and John left, Helena and the twins donned bathing suits and headed for the pool while Roberta and Colin relaxed in a cool shower and then stretched out on the bed Roberta would share with Helena. They talked quietly for a while and then fell asleep. When they woke, they found that Helena and the boys were in the living room watching TV and it was almost time to leave for the reservation.

They were all waiting in the lobby when Tressa and John arrived a few minutes early. Once again, Colin rode in the back of the pickup with Helena and the boys while Roberta rode up front. John had put some cushions in the back of the truck, so it was much more comfortable than before. The sun was setting as they left the lights of town and headed across open country. It grew quiet as the mysterious beauty of the desert captured even the boys with the glow of the setting sun casting shadows of intense changing colors. Roberta felt the energy flow through her and understood more than ever why her daughter was drawn to this place.

They arrived at the reservation to find a large crowd gathered around tables of food playing music and dancing. John introduced them to his parents, brothers and sisters who welcomed them with obvious sincerity. As Roberta and Colin sat quietly talking to John's parents, she was struck by a quality of peace and harmony that seemed to emanate from them. John's parents explained the wedding ceremony and the meaning of the ritual, and Roberta was struck by its simplicity and how much more meaningful it was than the wedding ceremonies she was accustomed to. She watched as Tressa and John danced a native dance, which his parents explained was to declare their intentions, to the sound of hauntingly beautiful music from flutes with drums beating a soft rhythm. Their love for each other was a tangible energy that surrounded them with a pulsing light of all the colors of the rainbow. She watched in fascination as the spirits of Indian ancestors danced around them to give their blessings. When the music stopped, Roberta blinked as though coming out of a trance and was surprised to see that the others had seemingly not noticed anything unusual. However, as Roberta's eyes met those of John's mother, she smiled slightly and nodded as though acknowledging the truth of what Roberta had seen. The celebration lasted until long after midnight, and John and Tressa drove them all back to the hotel. Roberta's dreams that night were filled with visions of Indian life when they were free to roam the country.

Tressa arrived at the hotel early the next day to take Roberta shopping before the afternoon heat. Helena joined them while Colin and the twins went off on their own. Roberta and Helena each bought lightweight dresses that seemed to float around their bodies for the wedding and several other simpler dresses to wear during the visit and cool cotton shirts and pants for Colin and the twins. Roberta told Tressa and Helena what she had seen the night before when Tressa and John had been dancing. Roberta felt closer to Tressa than she ever had even during the war when the two of them had been alone. The day was already quite warm when they returned to the hotel shortly after noon, and the twins were in the pool cooling off from their sightseeing. Helena joined the twins while Roberta, Colin and Tressa had lunch and talked quietly.

The days before the wedding passed quickly while they came to know the people on the reservation and understand more about their culture. They also saw what Tressa had meant about the problems with alcohol and lack of purpose of some of the people. Roberta understood Tressa's need to help them find pride in themselves and their special heritage. She watched with wonder as her daughter unwavering worked to help her adopted people.

The wedding was on the night of the fifth day after the party arrived from Ireland and was held outside under the full moon. Tressa wore a traditional native buckskin dress of soft, pure white covered with beautiful beading and matching moccasins with feathers and beads threaded through her hair. Roberta was sure that no bride had ever been so beautiful and tears coursed down her cheeks as Colin placed Tressa's hand in John's. The wedding celebration lasted all night and when dawn came, the bride and groom, according to tradition, slipped away for a week to an undisclosed location that had been prepared in advance before returning to begin their life together as part of the tribe. Tressa had explained this to her father and mother and said her goodbyes shortly before dawn. When the couple left, Roberta, Colin, Helena and the twins thanked everyone for their hospitality and John's brother drove them back to the hotel.

They slept late the next morning and spent the day relaxing and preparing for the trip to meet Mr. Hanson for the recording. Roberta had bought an Indian flute and played it softly as she and Colin sat on the balcony of the hotel looking out across the desert the night before they left. Though they were both sad to be leaving Tressa, they knew that she was blessed and would be happy here. The boys had enjoyed themselves very much learning to ride and hunt from the young Indian boys and looked forward to visiting in the future. Helena was very quiet, and Roberta knew that she was going to miss Tressa perhaps more than the rest of them would.

They caught a plane the following morning and then rented a car to drive while in town to do the recording. As usual, they had allowed an extra day in case of problems, so they were able to arrange a short visit with Judy. The following day they arrived early to find that Mr. Hanson had set aside the entire day for them. By this time, Mr. Hanson trusted

Roberta's judgment, so they got set up and began to record the music she had chosen. She had included several of the pieces written during the war as well a piece she had written for the Indian flute after their earlier visit to the states. Helena had a very lilting voice, and she sang several Celtic vocals backed by the clear young voices of the twins. Mr. Hanson was very happy with the result and even persuaded them to do a couple of extras as singles. The recording went very smoothly and within four days they were finished and ready to return home.

Colin had been much more relaxed on the flight from Arizona, but Roberta felt that he was not ready for the long flight over open water yet. He was obviously relieved when she suggested that they return home by ship. The ship was much faster than the others had been, so the trip took considerably less time than it had in the past. Helena and the boys played games, swam and enjoyed the company of other young people on board while Colin and Roberta were content to spend their days relaxing and enjoying the food and their nights making love and sharing their thoughts and feelings as the ship rocked gently.

They had taken many pictures on the trip and had them processed aboard ship. As they looked through the pictures taken on the reservation, Roberta saw that there were many balls of white light, which she knew were spirits. She had taken a picture of Tressa and John together before the wedding and was delighted to see that the camera had captured the energy field that surrounded them. She and Colin talked about these things but said nothing when other people remarked about the reflections from the flashbulb.

Chapter 32

As they drew closer to Ireland, the lightweight clothing was packed away for their next visit in favor of warmer woolen clothing. The ship docked on a rainy, cold day and they shivered as they made their way to the car where Francis waited to take them home. They arranged to have the instruments and luggage delivered and then crowded into the car. Because there were five of them, Francis had come alone and everyone else was waiting impatiently at Francis and Megan's. Hannah and Kate had helped Megan prepare a large meal, so they all gathered to talk about the trip and look at the pictures while they ate.

It was late by the time they had eaten and everything was cleared away, and Colin drove them home in Kate's car. Roberta sat on the edge of the seat to catch the first glimpse of the cottage, and her heart swelled as she saw that the elementals, fairies and angels had all turned out to welcome them home. Though she had felt a great attraction for the desert, nothing would ever replace the feeling of home she had whenever she returned to her beloved Ireland and the cottage.

They were busy that winter as life settled back into the routine of short days and long winter nights. Roberta painted using the pictures they had taken to help capture the illusive beauty and mystery of the desert. She and Colin also wrote music based on the sounds of the Indian music. She did several paintings of Tressa and John dancing with the energy field of their love and the spirits dancing around them and of the wedding itself. She did one of these paintings for Tressa and John, one to keep and one to send to the gallery. By spring she had done many paintings and watercolors, which she shipped to the gallery. She received a letter, and a check for a very large amount, a few weeks later from Mr. Logan who complimented her on her latest work.

The two families grew even closer now that Kate was living at the cottage. Roberta enjoyed the times that Francis and Megan visited with Maureen, Patrick and Helena, but Colin often retreated to Kate's room or the barn where it was quieter.

Now that Colin had recovered from the war, and the boys were older, he, Roberta and the twins often went to the pub in town where they all sang, danced and played music. The pub was soon filled with young girls whenever they went there, and Roberta watched as her precocious sons charmed the girls. Though the twins looked alike, Carlan was the more outgoing and adventurous of the two. Carlan reveled in attention from all the girls. Blair, however, singled out a quiet girl with a riot of red hair and masses of pale freckles. Roberta and Colin encouraged the boys to invite their friends to the cottage and began to dread weekends because the place was often overrun with young people. However, they agreed this was better than having to worry about where the boys were and what they were doing. Fortunately, there were always many people around to keep an eye on them.

Roberta and Colin visited Arizona when Tressa and John's son Jonathan was born just over a year after the wedding. As Roberta held her first grandchild, she became acutely aware of a sense of continuity and the natural flow of nature. They spent just over a week with Tressa and once again fell under the spell of the desert. It was easier to leave this time, as it was obvious that Tressa was happy and doing exactly what she was meant to do. They visited Judy for a few days on the way home, and Colin surprised Roberta by suggesting that they fly home. The flight home was uneventful, and Colin seemed completely relaxed once the plane was in the air. It was a beautiful sunny day when they returned to Ireland, and Roberta understood even more why it was called the emerald isle when she saw Ireland from the air for the first time.

That winter Kate caught a cold that turned into pneumonia, and despite the best medical care and energy healing passed peacefully away on a cold, blustery day in February. Roberta sat by the bedside watching as Kate joined Sean before they both faded away leaving the empty body behind. Colin had spent a great deal of time with his mother over the last few years and they had become very close, so Roberta watched him closely for signs of depression. Colin was quieter than usual, but as they sat by the fire the night after the funeral he told her that his mother and father had come together the night before to say goodbye. He smiled sadly as he remarked how young and happy they had looked. Roberta and Colin talked late into the night about the cycles of birth and rebirth and how much easier it is when you understand that death is only the end of one cycle and the beginning of another.

Now that they had more time, Roberta and Colin were able to become more involved in the community. They often helped out at the rehab center, which had slowly been converted to a long-term care facility. Roberta found herself wanting to understand more about the beliefs she had been taught as a child. She and Francis talked often about these things. She also began to study with the group of people who had been their friends over the years and realized how deeply instilled the beliefs were and how much her life had been shaped by these without her being aware of it. Colon joined the group and came to understand that what he had experienced during the war was something he had chosen for himself. With this knowledge he was able to finally release the fear and find peace at last.

Chapter 33

When the boys were 16, they formed a band with three of their male friends and a female vocalist and began playing for small affairs in the area. The band practiced at the cottage, and Roberta and Colin encouraged them to use a barn that was within sight of the house but far enough away so that they didn't have to hear them. They found it hard to believe that their sons could like such loud, abrasive music and hoped this was just a phase that they would outgrow. The boys had many girlfriends over the years as Roberta and Colin spent many nights waiting anxiously for them to come home unable to sleep until they knew the boys were safe. Roberta often wondered what idiot had ever said that it was easier raising boys than girls. They had never had to worry about Tressa.

The first rift between the two families came the year that Helena announced that she wanted to go to college in the states like Tressa had done after graduation. Megan was very angry and blamed Colin and Roberta because Helena wanted to leave home. Their son Patrick was attending a college in England where he was able to come home for weekends and holidays and planned to settle close to home when he finished college. Maureen had married just after graduation. She lived with her husband a few miles from the rehab hospital and was expecting her first child. Megan was certain that if Helena had never visited the states she would be content to stay home like the other two children. Francis tried to explain to her that each person has a purpose for their life and that things happen to help guide each of us toward that purpose but she refused to listen.

Helena left for college in West Virginia the following year. She flew home for the holidays each year and for summer vacations and Megan became resigned to the situation. Helena often talked to Roberta and Colin about the plight of the people who lived in the mountains. Roberta watched the young girl as she was torn between her desire to please her mother and the longing to follow her destiny.

Roberta and Colin had tried several times over the years to talk to the boys about college but were put off. When the boys were in their last year of school, they decided the time had come to settle this at last. After dinner one evening, Colin told the boys they needed to talk about college. It was quiet for a few minutes and then Carlan said they had decided not to go to college because they wanted to devote their time to the band. Several days of heated discussion followed before Colin finally relented. The following day Roberta contacted Mr. Harmon who arranged for the band to do a demo at a studio in Dublin. Colin had hoped this would put a stop to this nonsense but to his surprise and Roberta's Mr. Harmon liked the demo and helped the boys become established with a local recording company.

After graduation, the boys were seldom home as they pursued their musical careers. Blair married Ruth, the redhead he had met at the pub, the year following graduation. She often traveled with the band and kept Roberta and Colin up to date on their whereabouts. Carlan remained single and joked that he didn't want to be selfish by limiting himself to only one woman. Roberta and Colin enjoyed the peace and quiet when the boys were gone, but they also looked forward to the times when they were home and the house was once again filled with laughter and young people.

Francis and Megan flew to the states for Helena's graduation and Helena returned to Ireland with them. She came to see Roberta and Colin the following day and explained that she had decided to stay home and try to find some way to help people without causing her mother unhappiness by moving away. She soon got a job as a social worker and counselor in Dublin where she rented a small apartment.

With all of the children grown and living their own lives, the brothers and sisters once again became close. Roberta and Colin were always invited to Francis and Megan's for Sunday dinner where most, if not all the children and grandchildren were present. They occasionally accepted but usually left after only a couple of hours because of the chaos. Although Roberta sometimes found herself envying Francis and Megan for having their children close, she knew that it was important for each person to be able to make their own life choices. Helena often visited Roberta and Colin to enjoy the peace and energy of the cottage. She still talked wistfully about West Virginia but seemed to have made peace with her decision to remain close to the family.

Chapter 34

Roberta and Colin flew to the states at least once a year to visit Tressa, John and their two grandchildren Jonathan and Anna, and they always stopped on their way home to visit Judy. It was during one of these visits that Roberta and Judy decided one morning to drive out to the healing center where they had grown up. The center was closed and boarded up and looked as though no one had been there for a long time. It was obvious that the road was seldom used as Judy drove back to where the house and cabins had stood. The two women got out of the car and walked carefully around barely able to recognize the place that had once been their home. The only thing that was familiar was the little bridge across the stream.

An old man approached from the direction of a small cabin and asked what they were doing here. Roberta explained that they had grown up here and just wanted to visit their home. The man recognized them then and laughed as he told them he was Patrick who had worked for Anna and Robert. Roberta introduced Colin, and Patrick invited them back to the cabin. Patrick brought out a pitcher of lemonade, and they sat on the porch reliving the memories of those years so long ago when they had all been young. They talked about all that had happened in the years since. Patrick told them that the center had slowly become nothing more than a fancy hotel for the wealthy. The real healers left to work in other places leaving those who were only interested in making money. The children had all grown up and moved away to live their own lives. The business had already begun to fail when Brian died of a heart attack 15 years earlier, so Patrick closed the center. Brian's wife Doreen had moved to town to be close to her children and Patrick's wife Laura had died a couple of years ago.

He told them he had always felt guilty about what they had allowed to happen to Anna's dream until one day when he went for a walk and suddenly found himself at a strange stone cottage. Roberta smiled as he talked about what happened remembering her own experience at the stone cottage. He said Anna and Robert had appeared to him that day and assured him that everything had worked out as it was supposed to. As they sat on the porch sipping lemonade with friends, Roberta's parents and all those who had been a part of her life here appeared as though to welcome her home. She turned to Patrick to find that he was looking toward them with a smile on his face.

Roberta suddenly realized that the sun was getting low and it was getting late. She rose to leave with an apology to Patrick for having stayed so long. He assured them that he had enjoyed the visit and urged them to stay longer, but Judy explained that her husband would be home from work soon and would be worried if she wasn't there. Patrick hugged each of them and told them how happy he was to have seen them once again. Judy wrote her name and phone number on a piece of paper and told Patrick to call her anytime he wanted to talk or if he needed anything. Roberta, Judy and Colin talked on the way back about how people move in and out of our lives and how each of them has an impact on us. The two women remembered Patrick as the handsome young man who had always taken time to play with them and listen when they talked about the problems that had seemed so important then. They were both grateful for the opportunity they had been given to revisit the life they had shared as young girls.

Roberta and Colin returned home the next morning with an open invitation for Judy and Tom to visit them in Ireland whenever they could. They received a letter from Judy a few weeks later telling them that Patrick's daughter had found the number Judy left and called to let her know that Patrick had passed away. She also wrote that she and Tom planned to visit in the summer if that was all right with Roberta and Colin. Roberta answered immediately to thank Judy for letting her know about Patrick and to assure her that they looked forward to the visit. She called Francis that day to let him know about Patrick and about Judy's planned visit.

Chapter 35

Colin awoke one morning complaining of feeling dizzy and Roberta took him to Francis for a check up. When all the test results were back, Francis told them that Colin's blood pressure was very high and his EKG showed an abnormality, which Francis told them was probably a result of what he had undergone as a prisoner of war. He gave Colin a couple of prescriptions and told him to get light exercise by walking to keep his heart as strong as possible. After that, Roberta and Colin walked three miles every day except when it was too cold and wet. To keep the walk from being boring, they would drive to different places, park the car and then explore the surrounding countryside. They began to look forward to their adventures. On nice days, they would take painting supplies, a flute and lap harp and have a picnic as Roberta painted or joined Colin playing music.

They became closer than they had ever been as they shared the dreams of their youth and laughed or cried as they talked about their lives. Colin finally began to talk about the time when he had been a prisoner of war, and talking about it seemed to let him finally put it all behind him. He seemed more and more the man that Roberta had married and she fell in love all over again.

In June, Roberta received the long-awaited letter telling her that Judy and Tom would be arriving in two weeks. Roberta and Hannah cleaned the cottage from top to bottom and Colin helped the men who worked at the farm get the grounds surrounding the house perfect. They picked Judy and Tom up at the airport and then stopped at the cottage to drop off the luggage before driving to Francis and Megan's where they were all invited for dinner since the cottage was too small to hold everyone. As they approached the cottage, both Judy and Tom exclaimed how beautiful it was.

The dinner was very noisy and jubilant, and after dinner everyone drank coffee or tea and talked late into the night. Maureen was there with her husband and son as well as Patrick, Helena and the twins Carlan and Blair. As Roberta looked around the table, she was reminded of the dinners at the center and suspected from the looks on their faces that Francis and Judy were also remembering those days of so long ago. Before returning to the cottage for the night, plans were made for Francis and Megan to join Roberta, Colin, Judy and Tom the following day for sightseeing.

The next week was spent touring the countryside, exploring ruins and lunching in pubs where local people filled them in on the history and legends of the area. Francis often joined them on their explorations, but Megan begged off claiming to have too much to do. They walked miles each day and returned to the cottage each evening to sit talking quietly beside a warm fire after a hearty dinner until with eyes heavy they retired to their beds to dream of little people and tales of long ago.

The days flew by and all too soon it was time to say goodbye. Judy and Roberta wiped away tears as they promised to see each other again soon and to write often. Megan, Francis, Roberta and Colin stood waving as the plane lifted into the sky and turned to leave only when it was lost to view. On the drive back to the cottage, Francis thanked Roberta for maintaining the bonds with the past for them both and told her how much he had enjoyed the visit with Judy and Tom. He also told them that he and Judy had talked about Hank, and he knew now that there was nothing he could have done to help him. Roberta was very glad to hear this because she knew that Francis had blamed himself.

The twins had left on another tour two days after Judy and Tom arrived, so Roberta and Colin once again had the cottage to themselves. They planned to resume their walks the next morning, but Colin became tired after only a short distance and they returned home. Roberta assumed he was still tired from the visit and suggested they rest for a couple of days before trying again.

Roberta used this time to catch up chores around the cottage while Colin talked to the men about the farm work. Colin appeared to get stronger each day and when the third day turned out to be warm with bright sunshine, they set out across the field for a walk. They had walked only a short distance when Colin became very short of breath and fatigued, so after a brief rest they made their way slowly back home. This time Roberta knew something was wrong, and her hand shook as she reached for the phone to call Francis and ask if he could see Colin. Francis and Megan met them at the door when they arrived, and Megan led Roberta to the kitchen for a cup of tea. Colin and Francis joined them there a short time later and Francis told them that the medicine was no longer helping and there wasn't much that could be done. He suggested that Colin go into the hospital for testing to confirm this, but Colin refused and Roberta supported his decision.

Chapter 36

On the drive back to the little cottage, Roberta and Colin talked quietly about the best way to tell the children. They considered visiting Tressa, but when they spoke to Francis about it the next day, he didn't think that was a good idea. Roberta called Tressa to tell her about her father's condition and offered to wire money for a plane ticket if she was able to get away. Tressa called back the following day to say that she had arranged to be gone and asked them to send the money. Roberta also wrote to Judy and Tom to tell them how much she and Colin had enjoyed their visit and to tell them about Colin's health. When the twins returned home a couple of days later from their tour, Roberta and Colin told them the news. Blair and Ruth rented a small house close by and the twins told their manager that they wouldn't be going on tour for a while. Francis came by each day, and volunteered to pick Tressa up at the airport when she arrived the following week.

On nice days, Roberta and Colin took walks around the farm or sat outside where Colin played music or read while Roberta played music with him, painted or did household chores. The other family members and friends visited often, but Roberta limited the length of these visits because Colin tired so easily. After Tressa arrived, she often sat at her father's feet as they talked quietly for hours. Roberta didn't know what they talked about, but Colin seemed to be comforted by these times and that was all that mattered to her. At night Roberta and Colin lay cradled in each other's arms talking quietly until they fell asleep still nestled close together.

The twins stopped by for a visit just over a week after Tressa returned home. Roberta went to the kitchen to prepare lunch smiling happily as she listened to the teasing banter between Tressa and the twins while she worked. She was reaching for the plates to set the table when she felt a strange sensation as though something had torn inside her chest. It was several moments before she realized what had happened, but once she did she was surprised that after all the years she had worked so hard to maintain the bond between herself and Colin she didn't recognize immediately when it had finally broken. She walked slowing to the chair where Colin sat seemingly asleep. She kissed him gently and then turned with tears in her eyes to their children who had suddenly grown quiet. They all sat huddled together on the floor in the middle of the room comforting each other for a few moments and then Roberta rose to go to the phone and call Francis.

Two days later they made the now familiar trip to the family home where Colin's body was laid to rest with those of his ancestors. As they prepared to return home, Roberta looked up at the landing window and saw that Colin had joined his mother and father there to say goodbye. She moved to the car where Tressa took her hand and smiled, and Roberta knew that she had also seen them.

Roberta assured Tressa and the twins that she would be fine and they should get back to their lives; however, the children were reluctant to leave Roberta alone, and they had been discussing this when Helena came by that evening. Helena told Roberta she had come to ask if she could stay with her at the cottage. She told them she hated living in the city but didn't want to move back to her father and mother's home because it was always so chaotic. She said she had always loved the cottage and being with Roberta but had not wanted to ask while her uncle had been alive because she didn't want to intrude. As she talked, they all began to laugh and Roberta hurried to explain what they had been discussing when she arrived. Roberta had not really looked forward to being alone and gratefully invited Helena to move in as soon as possible; however she insisted that Francis and Megan be told before any plans were made. As Roberta lay in bed alone that night, she remembered her father telling her he had learned from her mother that what we need is always provided if we allow ourselves to be guided by the unseen force of our destiny. She lay for a long time in the dark with tears soaking the pillow beneath her head longing to be with those she had lost. Just as she was drifting off to sleep she saw a hazy outline of her mother, father and Colin standing in the corner of the room.

On Saturday they all helped Helena close her apartment and move everything to the cottage. There was a holiday spirit as they worked together laughing and teasing. As Roberta watched them, she felt a wave of gratitude wash over her for having these people in her life. Roberta had been concerned about how Megan would react to Helena moving to the cottage, but Francis and Megan brought lunch over, and Megan assured Roberta she was happy about the move.

Tressa left the following afternoon in a flurry of hugs and tears, and Roberta promised to make the trip soon to visit her. Carlan and Blair were leaving very early the next morning, so they said goodbye at the airport. Helena and Roberta returned to the cottage where Hannah had a good hot supper ready and a fire burned brightly to take the chill off the night. Helena and Roberta talked about family things and how things had worked out so well for both of them while they ate and cleaned the kitchen. Helena had to be up early the next morning to go to work, so they said goodnight and retired to their beds early.

Chapter 37

When Helena left for work and she was alone for the first time, Roberta found herself wandering from room to room starting one task only to leave it unfinished and start another. For the first time, the cottage that has always felt so snug and comforting felt very large and empty, and she was suddenly overwhelmed by loneliness. She slumped in the chair where Colin had always sat and tears streamed from her eyes. She didn't know how long she had sat like this when she became aware of a presence and looked up to see the gnome standing beside the chair. He talked to her about death and reminded her that no one is ever really gone. She felt ashamed and selfish as he reminded her of the extra years she and Colin had enjoyed together when all of the other men with him had died. Roberta felt her spirits lift as the gnome reminded her that life is a wonderful gift, and she began to feel hope for the future. After that whenever Roberta began feeling lonely, the gnome would appear to encourage her.

She slowly began to settle into a routine. She painted, wrote and played music and even helped out with chores on the farm. Helena insisted that Roberta join her and her friends for an evening in town occasionally, and Roberta realized she had missed having a social life. She also began to spend more time with the people from church and to join in activities. Helena went to church with her mother most of the time in order to avoid confrontation, but she and Roberta had long discussions in the evenings about spiritual matters. Helena loved to hear stories about the Center where Roberta and Francis grew up and the beliefs of their mother and father.

Francis often came by during the day for a visit on his way home from town and he and Roberta talked about the things she was learning and doing at church and about their childhood at the center. Roberta was surprised when Francis said one day that he envied her the chance to be involved in the things that they were both interested in. He said that Megan became very upset if he talked about things that he saw or sensed, and she had forbidden him to discuss any of what she called "this nonsense" around any of the children. As they talked, she realized that Francis was very lonely and she had been so busy with her own life she had been unaware of his unhappiness. Francis still worked at the rehab hospital, but it was really more of a nursing home now and there was little to do there. He said he had thought about selling it and setting up a small practice where he could really help people, but Megan liked things the way they were and didn't want him to do that.

Sean and Hannah came to the cottage one afternoon to talk to Roberta about the farm. They both seemed uncomfortable as though they wanted to say something that they dreaded having to say. Hannah finally told Roberta that Sean was having a lot of trouble with his back. She said they felt bad about leaving her, but they wanted to retire and move into town where they could be close to their children. Roberta thanked them for all the years they had been there to help with everything and assured them they shouldn't feel bad about wanting to be with their own family. Sean told her they planned to stay until the last of the crops were in and everything finished for the season. Sean finally rose to take care of his farm chores and left the two women talking about all the years they had shared life on the farm during the years when Colin had been missing and after he returned.

Francis stopped by on his way home that evening and Roberta told him about Sean and Hannah leaving. Roberta said she was considering selling off all of the land except the few acres around the house. She also told Francis she had been thinking about making a trip to visit Tressa in the late fall when the weather would be better. They were still talking about that when Helena got home and Francis had to leave. Roberta asked if Helena would be able to get time off from work and whether she would want to go with her. Helena was very excited at the prospect of visiting Tressa, and they sat up late that night talking about it.

Francis dropped by one Saturday to find Helena and Roberta busily going through their wardrobes to find suitable clothing for the trip. Francis made an effort to join in their revelry, but Roberta happened to look up unexpectedly and caught him off guard. Her heart ached as she realized how very unhappy he was. She thought how much Francis would enjoy Arizona and the culture of the people, and she turned suddenly to suggest that he come with them. For a brief moment, Francis' eyes came alive, but then the light went out and he said he couldn't go. Both women tried to convince him to join them, but Francis offered one excuse after another why he couldn't get away. During the days before they left on the trip, Helena and Roberta tried many times to get Francis to change his mind to no avail. They were both astounded when he arrived on the morning they were to leave to take them to the airport with suitcases packed and announced that he had changed his mind. He made light of the sudden decision, but Roberta sensed there was something he wasn't telling them. Nevertheless, the three of them set out on their adventure with spirits high.

Roberta had been doing a lot of painting since Colin's death and had shipped quite a few paintings to Mr. Logan during that time. Her paintings had changed over the years, and Mr. Logan had suggested she come by if she was in town, so they planned to stay in New York overnight. She had also written some new music, which she wanted to discuss with Mr. Hanson, and they planned to go by the studio after they visited with Judy on the way home.

Their plane arrived mid morning, and after a quick stop at the hotel to freshen up they took a taxi to the gallery. When they reached the gallery, they were taken immediately to Mr. Logan's office where he introduced them to his son who joined them for the delicious lunch Mr. Logan had arranged. During lunch Mr. Logan explained that because of his failing health his son had taken over the gallery. Roberta and Mr. Logan talked about the changes in her paintings over the years, and he told her she had developed quite a devoted following. He remarked that she seemed to be living the fairytale life of her paintings, as they talked about life in the little cottage in Ireland.

After lunch, Mr. Logan led them to a prominent area toward the center of the gallery where many of Roberta's paintings were displayed. As she stood looking at the paintings, it was as though her life was passing before her eyes. She was astounded as she saw how the different periods of her life and her own growth were so clearly reflected in the paintings. She also saw for the first time the prints and was very pleased with the quality and the knowledge that many more people were able to enjoy her paintings than would have been without the prints. When they turned to leave Mr. Logan pointed to the next wall where Roberta saw that a few of her mother's paintings still hung. He told her he had been offered a great deal for these over the years but just couldn't bear to part with them, although he had asked for and received permission to sell prints of them. When Mr. Logan invited them to dinner that evening, Roberta started to refuse as usual but surprised herself by accepting the invitation. She explained they would have to make it an early night because of the time difference and the fact that they had an early flight the following morning. Dinner that evening was at the Logan home and was very enjoyable. Mrs. Logan was a wonderful hostess and seemed genuinely interested as she asked about their life in Ireland. When Roberta embraced Mr. Logan at the end of the evening, she was very glad she had accepted the invitation because she knew this would be the last time she would ever see him.

Chapter 38

Tressa and John met them at the airport. Tressa had not known that Francis was coming, and she burst into tears of happiness when she saw her beloved uncle step off the plane. Tressa insisted that Roberta and Helena ride in the cab of the truck with John so that she could ride in the back with Francis. Roberta could see that Francis and Tressa were engaged in very serious conversation on the drive but was unable to hear what they were talking about as the old truck rattled over the rough roads. As she watched them, she was reminded how close they had been when Tressa was young. She felt again the sense of being an outsider, but she was glad that Francis had someone he could really talk to and chided herself for her jealousy. Roberta and Helena chatted with John for a while and then fell silent as the shadows lengthened and the desert once again cast its spell on them. Roberta watched in fascination as many generations of ancestors appeared and then faded from view.

They dropped their bags at the hotel and then drove to the reservation where John's relatives had prepared a large dinner in their honor. All of John's relatives were there to welcome them with food, music and entertainment. Time flew, and it was almost midnight when John drove them back to the hotel after they made arrangements to meet for lunch with Tressa and John at the reservation the following day.

Roberta awoke early and watched the sun rise over the desert before returning to bed where she slept until after 9 a.m. Francis joined Roberta and Helena at 10:00 for a light breakfast of coffee, toast and juice in the room that the two women shared and then left them to dress for the day. They drove to the reservation in a rental car Francis had arranged for that morning and arrived just in time for lunch. After lunch, Tressa took them on a tour of the clinic and classrooms and pointed out other things she had managed to obtain to improve the lives of those on the reservation. Roberta was overcome with pride and gave Tressa a warm hug as she expressed her amazement at how much one woman had been able to do. The last place that Tressa took them was the spiritual center and museum where members of the tribe came to listen as the elders told stories about the rituals, legends and spiritual beliefs of their people.

Roberta and Francis both enjoyed listening to the stories of the elders and spent some time each day in the spiritual center during their visit. They stayed in the hotel at night and drove to the reservation each morning where Francis helped out in the clinic and became happy again as he used his gifts to help people. Roberta spent much of her day with Tressa and the children. She enjoyed getting to know her grandchildren and found herself wishing she could be more a part of their lives. She felt especially drawn to Deanne, the youngest girl, who was very serious and reminded her of Tressa.

Roberta helped Tressa prepare meals and accompanied her as she fulfilled her duties. She discovered there was a rhythm and flow to life on the reservation and understood why Tressa was so happy with what some would consider so little. There was a rightness here that made worldly things seem trivial as one lived a life that drew its sustenance from something more important. When the day came to leave, Roberta felt as though she was leaving a very important part of herself behind and talked to John and Tressa about having the children visit her in Ireland.

Because Francis and Tressa had spent a great deal of time together, Roberta was surprised that he didn't seem at all reluctant to leave. He seemed to have a newfound sense of purpose, and she sensed that he had come to terms with something although she had no idea what it could be. They said their goodbyes at the reservation and Francis drove to the airport where they left the rental car and boarded a plane for the visit with Judy and Tom. Francis was unusually quiet on the flight but seemed happier than he had been in a long time.

Chapter 39

Francis again insisted on renting a car, so they called Judy from the airport to get directions. Judy was waiting excitedly when they reached the house and helped carry in the bags. She led them to the kitchen where coffee and tea were waiting. Tom arrived shortly after having picked up food on the way home from work, and they sat around the kitchen table catching up on all the news and looking at pictures of children and grandchildren.

Tom and Judy's children and grandchildren dropped in for visits and listened as Judy, Francis and Roberta talked about growing up at the center. Everyone listened raptly as they described the idyllic life, the healers who had worked at the center and the interesting subjects that had been taught there. The children grew quiet and wide-eyed as Francis described his playmates the fairies, gnomes, and other little people as well as his sister who had died shortly after she was born. The weekend passed quickly with stories that brought laughter and tears.

They had arrived on Friday and planned to leave Monday, but Francis surprised them all on Sunday night by saying he wanted to stay an extra day and visit the center. Helena was very excited about seeing the place she had heard so much about where her father and aunts had grown up and squirmed like a small child as they all drove out to the center early Monday morning.

It looked even more dilapidated than it had when Roberta and Judy had last been there. Weeds had taken over the once lovingly maintained grounds where an occasional flower could be seen struggling to compete. They had no interest in the buildings that had been built later but made their way to the main center where they were able to enter through a door that opened on the courtyard. They made their way carefully through the rubble talking about the memories of their childhood that came flooding back. When they reached the front entrance, Francis went immediately to the secluded corner where Anna had painted the picture of Diana. The others followed and just as he reached the spot, a cloud moved away and sunlight flooded in to light the picture that was still intact despite all the damage that surrounded it. He turned to say something and pointed to the other side of the room where Anna, Robert, Diana, Lilith, Aunt Helen and Uncle Ted appeared and then slowly fade away. Roberta went to stand beside Francis and put her hand in his as they both stood looking at the painting of the sister they had never had a chance to know.

They were startled by a sound and turned to find Helena pointing speechless toward the spot where the relatives had appeared and faded away. Francis and Roberta laughed as they teased Helena and Judy about being so white they looked more like ghosts than the real ghosts did. It was obvious that Helena was quite unnerved by the experience and Roberta moved to her side and put her arm protectively around her. Once they were back out in the sunshine, Helena seemed to regain some of her composure and was soon listening intently as the three of them talked about their memories of growing up here. They walked down the road to where the house had been and saw the cabin where Patrick had been living when Judy and Roberta had visited and looked out across the back of the property to the stream that had been dammed up to create a small lake. They talked about how nice the secluded glade had been on hot summer afternoons and what a shame it was that the trees had been cut down and the stream dammed up. They could see the orchard from where they stood and though it was neglected there was still fruit on the trees. Francis and Roberta didn't mention all of the little people that worked among the plants and trees and who seemed to welcome them back.

As they walked slowly back to the center where they had left the car, the relatives once again appeared and then slowly faded away. This time Helena didn't get upset and even asked about them. She listened with obvious interest as Francis and Roberta talked about the different relatives and Judy joined in occasionally to remind them of things they had forgotten. As they drove back to Judy's home, Helena remarked that she finally felt a part of the family since she had been able to see the things her father, aunt and cousin did. Francis teasingly asked if she was going to tell her mother about this when they got home, and they all laughed at the horrified look on her face at the very thought of having to talk to her mother about such things.

Roberta, Francis and Helena left the next morning to drive to the studio to see Mr. Hanson before flying back home. On reaching the studio, Roberta was saddened to learn that Mr. Hanson had died suddenly of a heart attack the year before. When Roberta told the young man who had bought the studio who she was, he excitedly invited them to lunch to talk about her music. He said he had discovered one of her earlier recordings recently and had tried to find her address in Mr. Hanson's files without success. Roberta had brought some of her music with her for Mr. Hanson to look over and when she showed it to the new owner Mr. Blake, he offered her what seemed like a small fortune to buy it. Although she was tempted, she remembered what had happened when she sold music before and refused. He then asked if she would record some of them. He had a harp and other instruments and Roberta had brought her flute. Roberta and Helena often played in the evenings and after a brief discussion they made arrangements to meet in two days to try a couple of pieces.

Since they weren't leaving right away, Roberta suggested they drive back to the town where they had lived and visit the pub where she had met Colin to see if any of her old friends were still there. By the time they arrived and got a hotel room, it was late afternoon, and Francis suggested they go to the restaurant where Lilith had taken Anna so many years ago. After many wrong turns, they found the restaurant and chose a table in a secluded spot. It soon became apparent that the clientele was not the same, but they enjoyed the meal and then drove to the pub that they had found earlier. The pub had not changed much in the years that Roberta had been gone, and she half expected Colin to walk through the door and sweep her into his arms. She sat lost in thought half listening to Helena and Francis talk about all that happened the last few days. A couple of older men were playing music, and Roberta suddenly sat upright as she recognized one of the earlier pieces she had recorded. She had her flute with her and decided to ask if she could join in. When she approached the men, she told them she had written the piece they were playing and asked if she could join them. One of the men got up so suddenly that he knocked his chair over, grabbed her and swung her around. Roberta was becoming alarmed until he asked if she didn't recognize her old friend Troy, and she recognized his voice. Roberta introduced Francis and Helena, and then joined the two men to play for a while. Before leaving that night, Roberta asked if Troy and his friend Dorian would join her in making another recording. They made arrangements to meet at the pub the following evening and go over some of the pieces she wanted to record.

The following morning Roberta called Mr. Blake to delay their meeting to allow time to practice with Troy and Dorian. They were to meet Troy and Dorian at the pub after the two men finished work, so the three of them ate a leisurely breakfast and then set off to explore the town. After wandering aimlessly for a while and reminiscing about their childhood, they unexpectedly found themselves on the street where Aunt Lilith's house had been. They were surprised when they reached the house to see that it was still there but was now a restaurant. Since it was close to noon, Francis suggested they stop for lunch. Everything had been completely restored, and as they sat at a table overlooking the courtyard Francis told them how he had stayed with Lilith while Anna and Robert went to the gallery showing and how much he had enjoyed the pool. A very frail, elderly woman sitting at the next table apologized for listening to their conversation and asked Francis if he had known Lilith. Francis said he had and introduced himself, Roberta and Helena. When the woman heard their names, she asked if they were Robert and Anna's children and on being told they were explained that she had been a healer at the center. She told them she liked to come here because it made her feel close to Lilith. They talked for a while about the center and about the years since they had left, and when the time came to leave, she hugged each of them warmly. They did some shopping for gifts to take home and then returned to the hotel to relax for a while and freshen up before going to dinner and the pub.

A large crowd gathered each night as they practiced the music Roberta had brought with her in preparation for the recording session. Francis joined Roberta and Helena when they sang, and Roberta realized for the first time that he had a very good voice. The owner of the pub was happy to have them because business was so good he had to order more supplies after the first night.

Both Troy and Dorian had arranged to take the following week off work, and they made plans to meet with Mr. Blake on Sunday to set up for a recording session early Monday morning. On Sunday afternoon, as they were setting up for the recording session the next day, Mr. Blake suggested the addition of chimes and provided a set for them to practice with. At 6 a.m. Monday morning they began recording and by the end of the second day had recorded 12 pieces. After some persuasion Francis had joined the others in the vocals and played the chimes. When they had finished the last recording, there was a moment of silence followed by resounding applause from the employees.

Mr. Blake surprised them by announcing that he had arranged for a press party that evening to introduce them and the recording. He had the recording playing during the party. For the first time, they were able to hear the music played and the reactions of those at the party. As Roberta listened to the people talking about the effect the music had on them, she felt overwhelming gratitude for the gift she had been given. After an hour, Mr. Blake introduced Roberta, Francis, Helena, Troy and Dorian. They were immediately flooded with requests for interviews and autographs and questions about plans for the future. It was an exciting evening, but they were all tired from the two-day recording session and glad to finally return to their hotel room.

Roberta, Francis and Helena had breakfast with Troy and Dorian the following morning before they returned home. Mr. Blake had given them a very large advance and Roberta gave half of it to Troy and Dorian. Tears filled her eyes as she said goodbye, and she invited them to visit her in Ireland.

It had been a grueling two days and Francis readily agreed when Roberta suggested they catch a train to New York rather than drive in order to relax before boarding the plane home.

They had a good dinner at the hotel before boarding the train in the late afternoon. The train left the station and moved into the open countryside as the sun sank low on the horizon casting long shadows across the landscape that rushed by outside the window. Francis sat lost in thought seemingly unaware of Roberta and Helena as they talked about everything they had experienced during the visit. Francis and Helena had grown closer during this time and Helena seemed confused at his apparent withdrawal as she tried to draw him into the conversation.

They had gotten a private room so they could stretch out, and the clack, clack of the wheels and the gentle sway of the train soon lulled the two women to sleep. Roberta awoke in the early dawn and watched as the night slowly gave way to another day and the sun rose triumphantly overhead. Francis and Helena stirred as the train slowed at the outskirts of New York and they all made preparations to leave the train. Since they had four hours until their plane was scheduled to leave, they ate a leisurely breakfast in the train station and then got a taxi to the airport. Francis seemed more at peace as they boarded the plane, but the light had faded once more from his eyes and it was obvious to Roberta that he dreaded returning home. Helena also noticed the difference and took his hand as though to comfort him.

Chapter 40

They arrived home early the next morning stiff, tired and longing for a warm, comfortable bed. The sun was still low on the horizon when they reached the cottage and they shivered in the chill as Francis helped carry in the luggage before kissing them goodbye and leaving to drive home. Roberta's heart ached as she saw how unhappy he was, and she and Helena talked about this as they prepared breakfast. After a quick bath to remove the grime of travel, they hurried to snuggle into their warm beds for some much-needed rest.

The two women awoke in the early afternoon ravenous and worked together to prepare a large meal and ate. Still suffering from jet lag, they unpacked and puttered with some laundry and household chores but were too tired to do much. They were preparing dinner when Francis drove up just before sunset looking very happy. He joined them in the kitchen and Roberta asked if he could stay for dinner. They were both stunned when he told them that he had already made arrangements to sell the hospital to a group of doctors. He said Megan was moving back to the family home and asked if he could stay at the cottage until everything was settled. Roberta assured him she was happy to have him stay with her, and they discussed the plans for the move and the sale while they ate and the women cleaned up the kitchen.

He told them about his conversation with Megan and the decision she had made to move back home. The two women were still absorbing all of this news when he announced that he was going back to the states. He said he had arranged to buy the property where the center had been and set up a practice there, in order to do what he was meant to do to fulfill his purpose and live the life he was meant to live.

As he talked, Roberta suddenly realized how much she relied on having him nearby now that Colin and the children were gone and how lonely it was going to be for her without him. She felt guilty for not being happier for him and only thinking selfishly about how his leaving was going to impact her life. She was trying valiantly to cope with this when Helena announced that she wanted to go with her father and work with him at the center. Roberta sat stunned as she realized that she would be completely alone for the first time in her life. Francis and Helena talked excitedly about their plans while Roberta smiled and tried to be happy for them. She went to bed early claiming fatigue and lay awake with tears running down her cheeks until she noticed a light in the corner of the room and saw her mother, father and Colin standing there watching her sadly. They told her how proud they were of her for keeping her pain to herself and trying to be happy for Francis and Helena. She was comforted somewhat by the knowledge that she would never truly be alone.

The next day, Francis and Helena met with Megan to take care of details, and Roberta was overwhelmed by loneliness. She sat in Colin's chair crying until she became aware of a presence and looked up to see the gnome standing beside her. He stayed with her until Francis and Megan returned, and in the following days whenever she was alone he kept her company. Helena gave her notice at work, and she and Francis made plans to leave in three weeks.

The twins arrived for a visit the next week. Roberta told them about Hannah and Sean moving into town and her plans to sell most of the land. The following day, Blair told Roberta that he and Ruth had been talking about settling down and raising a family and asked if they could live where Hannah and Sean had lived and run the farm. Although Roberta knew she would miss Francis and Helena, it was a relief to know she would still have family and even grandchildren close by. As Carlan teased his brother about becoming a farmer and a grandpa, Roberta sensed he was feeling the same sense of abandonment and loneliness she had felt at losing Francis. She knew that just as things had worked out for her with Blair and Ruth moving to the farm they would work out for Carlan if he allowed them to, but her heart ached for him, nonetheless.

After Francis and Helena left, Roberta found herself reaching for the phone many times to call Francis before realizing that he was no longer just a short distance away. She talked to them often and received letters every week that were full of their plans for the center and the work they were doing to restore the original building. Francis had encountered a great deal of red tape getting his license to practice in The States and had finally contacted some of his former colleagues for help. With their help and the fact that he had treated American soldiers in Ireland during the war, he finally managed to cut through the red tape. While they were waiting for this to be resolved, he and Helena were both working very hard to get the center ready and Judy and Tom visited often and helped out.

Roberta was torn between being glad they were so happy and her own feelings of abandonment and loneliness. Each letter urged her to come whenever she could, and she realized that they also missed her.

Blair and Ruth had moved in immediately and were settled by the time Francis and Helena left. Blair spent his days learning to farm while Ruth happily set about making a home for them. Sean and Hannah often came by, so that Sean could help Blair learn to run the farm while Hannah and Roberta visited, so life once again developed a comfortable rhythm.

In the spring, Ruth and Blair had announced that they were expecting a baby. Carlan was spending more and more time at the farm and joining Blair in the fields. He had established himself in his grandmother's old quarters and usually ate with Roberta. As Roberta spent more time with Carlan, she saw how much he was like his father had been before the war, and a strong bond developed between them. Blair and Carlan still practiced with the band and planned some tours during the winter months when work on the farm slowed down.

Roberta spent her time doing volunteer work, painting, writing music and tending the cottage and its grounds. She also spent many hours wandering the countryside remembering the days she and Colin had done this together. He often appeared as she sat painting or writing music on these outings.

Carlan began staying out a lot at night and Roberta was relieved when he announced he was interested in a girl named Mandy and wanted to bring her to meet the family. Arrangements were made for him to bring her to Sunday dinner and everyone spent days planning and preparing a special dinner. Roberta met them at the car to make Mandy feel welcome. When Carlan introduced them, Mandy put out her hand very formally and remarked what a quaint little cottage Roberta lived in. During dinner Roberta and Ruth searched for a topic that Mandy would be interested in, but all she seemed to want to talk about was the parties she had attended and the social standing of her friends. After dinner Blair offered to give Mandy a tour of the farm, but she remarked that would be a waste of time, as she had no interest in farming at all. Mandy noticed a painting Roberta had left to dry in the living room of a waterfall with gnomes, leprechauns and other little people dancing in the moonlight and fairies flying overhead and remarked how adorable it would be for a child's room. After what seemed like many hours Mandy announced that she had better be getting back to town, and Roberta walked out with them to say goodbye. Mandy thanked Roberta for the dinner and they both said it had been nice to meet the other as they shook hands. As their hands met, Roberta felt a dark foreboding wash over her. Roberta returned to the house where she assured Blair and Ruth that Mandy was really very nice and had only been nervous about meeting the family, but she was unable to convince herself.

Carlan continued to date Mandy who always made excuses whenever Roberta invited her to the cottage. Roberta's concern for her son continued to grow. He was staying out late and drinking heavily and she lay awake many nights unable to sleep until she finally heard him come home. She kept hoping that something would happen to break up the relationship, but after a year she expressed her concern to Blair who admitted he was also worried and agreed to have a talk with Carlan. Roberta never knew exactly what happened, but for the first time a serious rift existed between the twins. Carlan packed his things and announced he was moving into town where he could have fun and enjoy life with intelligent people instead of just being a dumb farmer.

Roberta's heart went out to both of her son's. Blair was deeply hurt by his brother's actions, but he had his wife and his son Sean who he had named after his grandfather. He withdrew from the band and contented himself with the farm and his family. It was Carlan that Roberta was worried about because of the life he had chosen to live. He had given her the phone number where he could be reached, so she kept in touch with him. At first, she called a couple of times each week, but then less and less as time went by. Their conversations were very stilted and though she asked each time, he refused to come for a visit and never invited her to visit him.

Chapter 41

The second year after Francis and Helena left, Roberta decided to make an extended visit to The States to visit Tressa and her family, Judy and of course Francis and Helena. She had arthritis and the cold, damp winters in Ireland were becoming very hard on her. Francis had suggested that a drier climate might be easier on her, so fall seemed like a good time to make the trip. Roberta made plans to leave in September. She was going to make a brief stop to visit with Francis, Helena and Judy for a couple of days and then continue on for a long visit with Tressa and her family before returning to the center where she would stay until spring.

She tried several times to call Carlan to tell him about her trip but was unable to reach him. After a month, she finally called the agent's number she had been given for emergencies and was told that they were no longer Carlan's agent, so she decided to drive into town and see if she could find Mandy. She found Mandy's parents who told her that Mandy and Carlan were no longer seeing each other and Mandy was on a European tour to recover from the relationship. They were very curt and told her to check the bars if she wanted to find her son.

Roberta had no idea where to begin to look and returned home hoping that Blair would have some suggestions. When she told Blair and Ruth what had happened, Blair kissed Ruth and said he had to go find his brother. Although he protested, Roberta insisted on going with him.

They had almost exhausted the places that Blair could think of when finally a bartender said he had seen Carlan talking to a disheveled looking man sitting at a table near the door. When they approached the man, he mistook Blair for Carlan and started talking about how much better he looked. Blair explained that Carlan was his twin brother and that he and their mother were trying to find him. The man was reluctant to get involved at first, but was finally convinced to help them with the offer of a generous reward. He guided them to several places, each of which was worse than the one before. Roberta's concern grew as she saw the places that her son had been frequenting. The fourth place was so dirty and smelled so bad that she hesitated to even go in, but concern for her son drove her on. As they made their way around the room, her eyes were drawn to a slumped form in a corner. She made her way though the dirty throng with Blair at her side. As they approached, Carlan raised his head and mumbled in a drunken stupor. Without a word, Blair and Roberta got on each side and supporting Carlan between them led him out to the car.

Roberta wanted to take Carlan home, but Blair finally convinced her that he would be better off in a hospital. Roberta knew several of the doctors who had bought the hospital from Francis, so they took him there. When they explained who they were, the doctor on duty agreed to admit Carlan. Blair took him to a shower, stripped his filthy clothes, scrubbed him and dressed him in a clean gown before the doctor examined him. When the doctor finished his examination, he told Roberta and Blair that Carlan's condition was serious but he would recover if he gave up the drugs. Blair didn't seem surprised, and he told Roberta that he had suspected Carlan did drugs when he was still in the band.

In the days that followed, Roberta stayed by Carlan's side as he went through withdrawal from drugs and alcohol. They learned that Carlan had spent all of the money he had saved over the years on alcohol, drugs and partying and when the money was gone Mandy had left. After she left, he drank and did drugs even more until the agency finally dropped him for showing up too stoned to perform a few weeks earlier. Since then, he had lived on the street and spent his royalty checks on drugs and alcohol.

Roberta used the healing techniques she had learned years earlier to balance his energy and heal his mind as well as his body. As she was able to reach him on a deep level, she realized how frightened and alone he felt. After a week, Roberta was able to take Carlan home. Blair had visited him every day in the hospital and when they reached the house, Blair and Ruth were waiting to welcome him. The doctor had given Roberta medication to help Carlan with the withdrawal. They all talked openly about what had happened and Carlan was aware that while the family did not approve of what he had done, they loved him and were willing to help in any way they could.

As the time drew close for Roberta to leave, she asked Carlan to join her. She admitted that she was afraid to leave him alone but said she also felt the change would be good for him. Carlan was hesitant to leave the security of the cottage, but Roberta pointed out that they would be with family who knew what had happened and wanted him to come. He finally agreed and even began to look forward to the trip.

Chapter 42

As they drove away to go to the airport, Roberta looked back at the cottage and felt a pang of sadness knowing she would be gone for so long. However, the weather was cold, wet and windy; and she was glad to know that they would soon be in a milder climate. The rift between Blair and Carlan had healed, and they talked freely and joked about Carlan bringing home a Yankee wife like dad did. Ruth had stayed home with Sean because he had a slight cold, so Roberta sat alone in the back seat listening to her sons' banter and thinking about the other trips she had made between the states and Ireland beginning with the first time when she had seen and fallen in love with her adopted country and the time she had returned as a bride.

The plane was a little late arriving in New York, but they were able to make the connection for another plane that would take them to where Francis would be waiting. As the plane lifted into the sky, Roberta marveled at the beauty of her native land. The landscape was a riot of fall color. She told Carlan she had never really appreciated this until she was away for a while and saw it with fresh eyes. Her eyes misted as Carlan kissed her on the cheek and told her we never appreciate the special things that are a part of our everyday life.

Francis and Helena were waiting when the plane landed, and the ride back to the center was filled with laughter and noise with everyone talking trying to get caught up on the news. Judy and Tom had fixed a large meal and were waiting at the center with some of their family. When Francis led the way into the center, Roberta stopped frozen. It looked like it had all those years ago with the big table loaded with food, and the air filled with the sound of laughter and music. Roberta caught a movement in the courtyard and looked up to see that all of the relatives had gathered to welcome them before slowly fading away. Helena laughed as she pointed to Carlan who looked as though he wanted to run but didn't know which way to go. As they talked about how frightened she had been the first time, Carlan seemed to relax a little. When dinner was finished, everyone helped clean up.

Because Francis had told Roberta that the clinic was becoming quite busy, she had planned her arrival on a Saturday evening in order for them to have a day without any patients. Judy and Tom were staying over, so they all sat around the table after the others left talking until the time difference caught up with Roberta and Carlan. Roberta and Carlan were to share rooms with Helena and Francis, and everyone laughed as Carlan admitted he was relieved to be sharing a room with his uncle just in case the relatives decided to show up again.

The next morning, everyone pitched in again preparing breakfast and cleaning up afterwards. Francis told Roberta that shortly after he opened his clinic, several people came out who had known their parents. He and Helena had been attending church with them and Helena had taken some classes on different subjects. As he talked about the things he was doing, Roberta could see the peace and sense of purpose he had now. She was reminded of what life had been like growing up here. She had taken that life for granted, and for the first time she realized how special it had been and how much she missed it.

Francis showed them around the grounds after breakfast. He had hired people to care for the grounds and orchard and had them remove the dam from the little stream and had the bridge repaired. Most of the cabins had been torn down, but two of the larger ones were being repaired. Francis said he and Helena planned to live in one of them, and he told Roberta that she was welcome to use the other cabin any time she wished. Roberta saw that a rather large community of little people lived beside the stream, and she sat with Francis on the bank watching them as fairies flew overhead.

The day seemed to fly as they all got caught up with the news and renewed their bonds. They had an early dinner so that Judy and Tom could get back home before it grew too late. After they left, Roberta and Francis bundled up and went outside to sit in a swing while Helena and Carlan listened to music and talked. Roberta and Francis talked about Carlan. She was concerned because there were times when she sensed he was drawn back to the drugs and alcohol. Francis said he had also sensed this, but all they could do was be there for him if he needed them. He offered to have Carlan stay with them while Roberta visited Tressa, but Roberta explained she was hoping Tressa might be able to help him.

The next day was busy as Francis was closing the clinic early in order to take Roberta and Carlan to the airport to catch their plane in the afternoon. Francis surprised Roberta by bringing out a harp, which she played while Carlan helped Helena. They all worked well as a team and the patients were seen in plenty of time for them to leave for the airport.

As the plane lifted off, Roberta felt Carlan tense beside her and saw that the relatives were standing behind Francis and Helena as they waved goodbye. She laughed softly as he whispered that he didn't think he would ever get use to them showing up like that.

Chapter 43

John and Tressa met them at the airport driving the same old truck. Tressa insisted that Roberta sit in the cab of the truck with John while she sat in the back with Carlan. Roberta looked back once and saw that Tressa had her arms around Carlan with his head in her lap and was very glad that he had come with her. There was something very right about bouncing along the rough road on the reservation in the old truck as John talked about Tressa and the children. When the truck stopped, the children ran forward to greet them. Once again, Roberta was struck by how much Deanna was like Tressa had been as a child.

There was a gathering that evening, and it seemed that the entire reservation had turned out to welcome them with food, dancing and drinking. Roberta became concerned when she saw that some of the people were drinking quite heavily but relaxed as Tressa stayed with Carlan, and he didn't seem to be interested in drinking.

As they sat at the table after breakfast the next morning, Tressa handed Roberta a package wrapped in plain brown paper. Roberta unwrapped it while Tressa explained that she had starting writing down the stories of the elders because she was afraid they would be forgotten. She had mentioned this to a friend one day who in turn had told a friend of hers who offered to publish the stories in a book. Sales had been promising, and Tressa was working on another book, which the publisher had already offered to publish. Over the next few days, Tressa pointed out the things that she had been able to do for the people on the reservation with the money from the book. Roberta was filled with pride and wonder for this daughter of hers.

Roberta and Carlan quickly became immersed in the daily routine of Tressa's family and life on the reservation. Roberta enjoyed sitting in the warm sun letting it ease the stiffness in her joints as she became lost in the sense of timelessness she felt here. Tressa spent a great deal of time with Carlan, and Roberta had more time with her son-in-law and grandchildren. She and John often sat outside in the evenings talking while the children played as the shadows lengthened and the sinking sun painted the landscape in soft shades of tan, pink and orange. She never tired of the beauty of the desert, which was in such stark contrast to the rich green of her beloved Ireland. As John talked about his heritage and life, she saw the quiet strength and deep spirituality that had captivated Tressa.

Roberta had tried for years to get Tressa, John and the children to visit her in Ireland but there had always been the excuse of not enough money. Now that there was money from the book, she brought this up again; however, Tressa insisted that the money from the books should be for the entire reservation. The children were fascinated when Roberta talked about Ireland and showed them pictures, and Roberta pointed out that they should be aware of their heritage from both sides of the family. John had never traveled, and he surprised them all when he agreed with Roberta telling them how he envied Tressa when she talked about the places she had been and the different things she had seen. He said he wanted his children to know about more than just life on the reservation. Between the two of them, they finally convinced Tressa to use some of the proceeds for a family trip to Ireland the following summer while the children were out of school. They also talked about them visiting the center during the winter holidays.

The two weeks of their visit passed quickly, but Roberta was able to leave happy with the knowledge that she would see them again soon. As she held Tressa in her arms saying goodbye, she felt a strengthening of the bond between them and found herself remembering those years when Colin had been missing. As she kissed Tressa on the cheek and moved to leave, she saw tears welling in Tressa's eyes and knew that she had shared the experience.

As the plane left the earth behind and rose to ride above the clouds, Carlan thanked his mother for bringing him on the trip. For the first time, he talked about Mandy and the lifestyle he had led with her. He talked about how deserted and lonely he had felt when Blair and Ruth moved to the farm to start a life of their own. He said that this trip had taught him about real relationships as the family had shown their support without condemnation. They were so engrossed in their conversation that it seemed only minutes before the plane was landing.

Chapter 44

It was Saturday evening when they arrived and the clinic was closed, so Francis suggested they stop to eat in town before returning to the center. He took them to a restaurant that the people from church frequented, and they were invited to join a group at a large table in the back. The talk soon turned to astrology, energy healing and the things Roberta had grown up with. Carlan seemed fascinated as he listened with a quizzical look and asked questions. Roberta realized that she had taken these things so much for granted that she had neglected to teach her sons. As she thought back over the years, she realized that it was only after Colin died and the boys were grown that she once again became actively involved with her earlier teachings. She was feeling very guilty about this when Carlan remarked he wished he had known about these things earlier, and one of the women told him that he had not been ready before and that things come to us when we are ready for them. Roberta's feeling of guilt vanished as she remembered her father quoting her mother who said we always get what we need when we need it.

The repair work on the first of the two cabins was completed a few days after Roberta and Carlan returned from Arizona, and the four of them moved Francis and Helena to the cabin, which was furnished with odds and ends from the hotel. Two weeks later Roberta and Carlan moved into the other cabin. By Thanksgiving, all of the rooms at the center were available for members of the church to do healing or teach classes there. Roberta began to practice healing again and regularly played the harp or flute in the evenings after dinner. Without planning, they had fallen into the habit of all eating together at the center and then walking together to the cabins as they had when they were children. When the weather permitted, they sat on the porch talking and watching the elementals until their eyes grew heavy with sleep.

Everyone pitched in to decorate the center for Thanksgiving. Judy and Tom came out the day before Thanksgiving to help prepare the large dinner for the family and any members of the church who wished to join them. They were joined by many of the church members who also came to help, and the day took on a festive air. Wonderful smells filled the air, and the pantry and cooler were soon filled to their limit with wonderful things awaiting the final touches the next day. Judy and Tom stayed over that night and everyone was up early to put the turkeys in the oven and then eat a leisurely breakfast. At noon others began to arrive, and by 2 p.m. the tables were groaning under a wonderful array of food.

As they sat around the table eating and enjoying the company, Roberta was reminded of those days long ago, and her eyes misted with tears as waves of nostalgia washed over her. She looked up to find that Francis was watching her and knew that he was also remembering the days of their youth.

When everyone had eaten as much as they possibly could and the food was put away or covered with cloths, the family returned to their cabins to relax while others stretched out on mattresses and linens left over from earlier times that had been spread on the floor throughout the building. That evening everyone once again met to eat leftovers. Everyone was lazy from eating so much and many chose to stay overnight and sleep on the mattresses. Those who left to return home were loaded down with leftovers to take with them. Most of the others left the following morning, but Tom and Judy stayed for the entire weekend and helped out at the clinic on Saturday.

In the weeks that followed, Carlan seemed happier than he had ever been and Roberta was surprised to see how hard he studied and worked with Francis to develop his sensitivity and healing skills. He had always been the irresponsible twin, and she found it difficult to believe he would stick with this. As she sat alone on the porch enjoying the warmth of the sun one afternoon and thinking about Carlan, her father and mother appeared. They told her that Carlan had always possessed a great gift, but he had to be disappointed in things of the world before he would be ready to accept his heritage. They also pointed out that the twins had learned a lot just by being around her and Frances and hearing them talk about the wonders of their special world.

Roberta was alarmed as she saw Carlan running toward the cabin one afternoon obviously very excited. She had trouble understanding him as he began to tell her about seeing and talking to his father. When she finally got him to calm down so that she could understand what he was saying, she realized that he was telling her about his experience with the magical stone cottage. As he talked about suddenly finding himself at a strange cottage, Roberta remembered the day she had been so distraught over the death of her uncle and had her own experience with the cottage. She smiled as he told her about the book and his father explaining about death. They laughed together as he talked about the wonders he was now able to see all around him. As they walked to the clinic to help prepare dinner, Roberta told him about the years when his father had been missing.

Tressa, John and the children came to stay for a week at Christmas. Tressa had finished her second book and was surprised by the amount of money the two books were earning. She was planning to visit other reservations to gather stories for a third book. Roberta sensed a difference in the relationship between Carlan and Tressa now that he understood and could share the wonders of Tressa's life.

Tom, Judy and their children and grandchildren joined them on Christmas Eve. There had been a light snow the night before and the younger members of the family played in the snow and sledded down the hill. That night they gathered at the clinic for dinner as usual and to exchange gifts. Those who were staying at the clinic overnight joined the others to walk to the cabins. A full moon turned the landscape into a sparkling wonderland and the children grew quiet and stared at the fairies flying through the air, the little people who lived throughout the grounds and the angels that surrounded the group. Even those who were accustomed to seeing this world were caught up in the beauty and magic of the night. Once at the cabins, they parted with whispered goodnights as though unwilling to break the spell and went to their beds to dream of a land of magic and wonder.

On Christmas morning, the children were eager to open their gifts and were up before the sun. The cabins were too small for everyone, so the gifts had been left at the clinic, and everyone shivered as they bundled up and then hurried to the clinic laughing and throwing snowballs.

The week flew by and all too soon it was time to say goodbye to Tressa and her family. Everyone gathered at the clinic for a leisurely breakfast. All eyes glistened with tears as the group huddled together in the crisp winter air to wave goodbye until the car was lost to view. Roberta would be returning to Ireland in the spring. She planned to spend a few days at the clinic and then a long visit with Tressa and her family in Arizona when she returned in the fall.

Chapter 45

Even though the winter was very cold, Roberta's arthritis was better with the drier climate and a tonic Francis mixed for her of lemon juice, honey and some secret ingredients. She spent the cold winter days working on music at the clinic and helping out when needed. In the evening she often went to the pub where she, Troy and Dorian played and made changes to the music she had written in preparation for another recording. She had talked to Mr. Blake and made tentative plans to make another recording when she returned from her trip to Arizona the following year. Carlan, Francis and Helena usually accompanied her and joined the group to play or sing. Everyone usually had a beer or two and Roberta had worried at first about Carlan, but he enjoyed himself without showing any tendency to lose control.

Francis had kept all of their father's notebooks and on returning to the clinic had hired a young man named Tony to take care of the grounds and help with a small garden of medicinal foods and herbs. Since Tony was single, he usually joined them for lunch and dinner and had also joined them for the holidays. He had asked Francis for permission to repair one of the cabins and to live there. Francis readily agreed, and he and Carlan helped Tony with the repairs. Roberta noticed during the holidays that Helena seemed to always be seated next to Tony. As the winter progressed it was obvious that a relationship had developed between the two, and Roberta was not surprised when Helena and Tony announced in March that they were engaged.

Tony's father had passed away the year before, and his only family was his mother Sarah and sister Alene. Tony brought his mother and sister to meet Helena and her family the Sunday after the announcement and they helped with the plans. It was decided to have a simple ceremony in May before Roberta left for Ireland. The ceremony was to be held outside if the weather permitted, but the clinic was large enough to accommodate everyone if it had to be held indoors. Helena had confided in Tressa at Christmas and gotten her to agree to be maid of honor, and Roberta was happily surprised to learn that she was going to see her daughter again before she left for Ireland.

Helena had written to her mother to tell her the news and asked her to come to the wedding. To everyone's surprise Megan called as soon as she got the letter and said she would love to come, so once the date was decided on Helena called to let her mother know. Megan said she would like to come a week before the wedding to help out, and Helena assured her that would be fine as there was plenty of room for her to stay at the clinic.

During the months before the wedding, Sarah often stayed with Tony and joined the others at the clinic where she helped with the cooking and cleaning. Francis had talked about hiring someone to help out, and he talked to Tony and Helena about offering Sarah the job. Helena said that she enjoyed having Sarah there and it would make her very happy. Tony thanked Francis and said Sarah had confided to him how much she enjoyed being at the clinic because she had been so lonely before. That night at dinner, Francis invited Sarah to live and work at the clinic. Sarah was so overcome it was a few minutes before she was able to tell Francis that nothing would make her happier than to live and work at the clinic with all of the wonderful people there. She said she had been looking for a job without success and this was the answer to a prayer. There was an impromptu celebration as everyone welcomed Sarah to the group. It was decided that she would share Tony's cabin until the wedding. After the wedding, Sarah would share the cabin with Roberta and Carlan would take Helena's room with Francis.

As the weather grew milder, Roberta often sat on the porch of the cabin to work on her music and even did some painting. Carlan joined her one beautiful April day and told her that he was not going back to Ireland with her. He said he had talked to Francis and was going to work at the clinic and continue to study. He said he did plan to visit her and Blair for a couple of weeks in the summer but he felt this was his home now. He then told her about a plan he and Francis had discussed for him to get formal training in holistic medicine through a university so that he could legally do more at clinic. Roberta had wondered if he would be returning with her but had not asked because she didn't want to put any pressure on him. They talked about the things he would be studying, and she was happy to see how informed and excited he was.

Megan arrived the first week in May and Francis moved his things to one of the rooms at the clinic so that she and Helena could be together. Megan seemed nervous at first, but everyone made an effort to make her feel welcome, and she soon joined in the excitement of getting ready for the wedding. She helped Sarah with the cleaning and cooking, and they became friends as they exchanged Irish and American recipes and argued good-naturedly about which was best. Roberta often saw Megan watching Francis when he wasn't looking and realized that she still loved him. She overheard Megan and Francis talking one night about how much they missed the early years of their marriage when they had been so happy. Megan said she had been wrong and that she envied Francis the life he had here at the clinic. The next day Francis moved his things back to the cabin and told everyone that Megan had decided to stay. Francis told Roberta a few days later that Megan had seen the spirits of her father, mother and Colin in the family home and she was no longer afraid of the things Francis and Roberta believed and knew they were right.

Tressa arrived the day after Megan and shared the cabin with Roberta and Carlan. Although it was good to see her two children together laughing and teasing again, Roberta found herself feeling nostalgic and longing for someone to share the little things of life with. As she laid in bed that night feeling lonely and sad, Colin appeared by the bed as though to remind her that he had never really left.

Francis surprised the bride and groom at dinner the night before the wedding with tickets and reservations for an island get-away for a week so that they could have some privacy. Sarah and Megan had helped them pack after dinner, as they would only have a couple of hours after the service to catch the plane in order to be on the island that night.

The day of the wedding was perfect, and the wedding was everything that they had all hoped it would be. The men had built an arbor for the bride, groom and minister to stand under and it was covered with flowers. A light rain had fallen the night before and left everything clean and glistening in the sunlight. Seats were arranged facing the arbor and overlooking the small stream with a flower-strewn carpet for the bride to walk on to the arbor preceded by her maid of honor. Roberta saw that the elementals had turned out in force to celebrate the day and silently thanked them for their hard work in making everything so wonderful.

The reception after the ceremony was held in the clinic with all the doors open into the courtyard to allow for better flow. The couple slipped away after cutting the cake to change and leave for their trip. When they drove past the clinic on their way to the airport, everyone was waiting to wave and shout goodbye. It was early evening before the guests left and those of the wedding party began to put things away. Everyone was tired, so they decided to leave most of the clean up for the morning and just sat around the large table in the clinic talking and enjoying the afterglow of the day. The relatives had appeared throughout the day to share in the joy. Everyone laughed at Carlan when he confided to the family members during the reception that he still found it a little disconcerting when they popped in and out like that en masse.

Francis had closed the clinic on Saturday for the wedding, and they were surprised when a large group from the church came to help with the clean up on Sunday. Roberta noticed that several of the women didn't seem too happy about Megan's presence, and she realized that they had hoped to catch Francis for themselves. As they worked together, the day took on the air of a party, and when the work was done they had an early dinner before the volunteers returned home.

As they walked back to cabins that night, Francis told them that he and Megan were going to be married again and that was why he had closed the clinic on Monday. He had already made arrangements with the minister for a very simple ceremony the next day. Roberta raised the question about where Carlan was going to stay since Sarah was moving into their cabin and Francis and Megan would want to be alone. Sarah assured them that he could share the cabin with her since he had his own room, and he had become like a son to her.

Francis and Megan's wedding the next day was very simple with only the family present and no fanfare. They stood under the same arbor to say their vows, and then everyone had a simple dinner at the large table as usual. Megan had asked for Roberta's forgiveness for the past and they had grown close in the time before the wedding.

Tressa left the following day, and Roberta prepared for her return to Ireland. She was to leave the following Saturday, and as the time grew close she was torn between wanting to see her other son, the beautiful little cottage and her beloved Ireland and her reluctance to leave her loved ones at the clinic. Francis sensed her turmoil and took her for a walk one afternoon. They talked about all the things they had shared both here and in Ireland. By the time they returned from the walk, Roberta was once again looking forward to returning home to Ireland.

Carlan offered to drive her to the airport on Saturday afternoon, so she said goodbye to everyone else at the clinic. On the drive, Carlan told her that Francis had arranged for him to get into a two-year holistic medicine program that started in June. He seemed very sure of himself and looking forward to the future as he talked about the different things he would be studying, and as the plane lifted into the sky Roberta said a prayer of gratitude.

Chapter 46

It was dark as the plane lifted into the air and turned its nose northeastward. As they flew into the night, lights were dimmed, a hush fell over the cabin, and Roberta fell asleep thinking about the lush green of Ireland. She awoke to sunlight streaming through the window and caught teasing glimpses of the beautiful green jewel below through the mists that shrouded it in mystery. As the plane descended through the mist, her heart swelled with happiness to be back home. She gathered her belongings eager to be off the plane and on her way to her little cottage and her family there.

She had not told Blair when she was arriving because she wanted some time alone to become reacquainted with her adopted homeland. She rented a car at the airport and drove leisurely through the countryside allowing herself to fall under Ireland's spell stopping several times to drink in its beauty. When she reached the drive to the cottage, she got out of the car and stood for a while looking at the cottage nestled among the trees and flowers, the rocky landscape and stone fences. Smoke rose in the air from fires that had been lit to dispel the early morning chill, and she shivered suddenly in the unaccustomed chill as she hurried back to the warmth of the car and drove into the yard. The car rolled to a stop beside the cottage and Blair stepped into the yard from the dwelling where he and Ruth lived. He yelled to let Ruth know that Roberta was home and then hurried to the car, lifted his mother and swung her as he chided her for not letting them know she was arriving that day.

Roberta looked up to see Ruth walking toward them and teased them about keeping secrets of their own, as Ruth appeared to be very close to giving her another grandchild. Ruth ushered Roberta into their quarters while Blair took her bags into the cottage, turned up the heat and built a fire to take the chill off. Ruth brought Roberta a cup of tea and they sat by the fire talking about the baby and catching up on the local news. Sean had been shy at first but finally allowed Roberta to pick him up and snuggled onto her lap where he fell asleep while they talked. When Blair returned, she told them about the clinic, Helena's wedding, and the surprise re-marriage of Francis and Megan the following day. Carlan had called to tell Blair that he wasn't coming back with Roberta, and Blair was obviously relieved when Roberta confirmed how well Carlan was doing and told them of his plans for the future.

Ruth fixed breakfast while they talked, interrupting to ask questions of her own from time to time. Roberta had been surprised to see that Blair and Ruth had changed their living quarters from what had been an outbuilding into a very nice home, and she complimented them on what had obviously been a lot of hard work. Blair explained that he had kept a couple of the best men busy working on the house over the winter so that they would not leave. He told her about plans he had for building hot houses to grow some fresh vegetables in the winter in order to provide work for the men and add income. By the time they had eaten and caught up on all the news, Roberta was very tired and longed for a warm bath and a nap. On the way to the cottage, she stopped to watch the elementals and to thank them for taking care of everything.

Ruth and Blair had made certain the cottage was clean and ready for her return even to stocking the refrigerator. She took a warm bath and then sat for a few minutes in Colin's chair before the fire to let the cottage settle around her once again. Her eyes grew heavy as the glow of the fire warmed her body, and she finally made her way to bed where she snuggled beneath a large downy comforter.

Roberta awoke shortly after noon and stretched enjoying the comfort of the warm bed before throwing on a robe and putting the kettle to boil for a cup of tea. When it was ready, she took her cup of tea and sat outside in the warm afternoon sunshine. The vines that grew up the side of the cottage were covered with blooms that filled the air with their heady perfume. She could hear the sounds of the men working in the field and Ruth singing to Sean as she went about her housework. Roberta's thoughts turned to those days when she and Colin had spent so much time sitting in this same spot, and she smiled as she saw him appear briefly and then slowly fade away as she rose to go back inside.

Francis had given her a packet of herbs with instructions on how to mix them with lemon juice and honey for her arthritis. She mixed a batch according to the instructions and put it on the stove to steep while she unpacked and did some laundry. When she had finished her chores, she walked over to say hello to Ruth and Sean and to thank Ruth for taking such good care of the cottage and making it ready for her return. She played with Sean and helped Ruth with dinner while they chatted. When Blair came in from work they talked for a while and then Roberta rose to leave, but Ruth insisted that she stay for dinner.

Over dinner, they talked about the finances of the farm and Blair's plans for the future and then talk turned to the clinic. Roberta had been hesitant to talk too much about things at the clinic, but Blair seemed very interested and asked a lot of questions. He told her he often saw his father and grandparents, and Roberta had them both laughing when she told them about the first time Carlan saw the relatives. Ruth was very quiet at first, but as Roberta talked about the clinic and the things being done there she seemed more relaxed and joined in the conversation. Roberta was still feeling the effects of the time change and returned to the cottage as soon as the dishes were done. As she sat before the fire drinking the tonic, she suddenly felt very lonely and longed for the comfort of Colin's arms once again. Through the tears that filled her eyes, she saw that the gnome had once again come to comfort her. As he talked to her about the wonders of life, the room filled with elementals, fairies flew overhead, loneliness faded, and she was filled with joy and enthusiasm for the future once again. She fell asleep in the chair before the fire and awoke a short while later to stumble sleepily to her bed.

Chapter 47

Tressa, John and the children arrived for a visit two weeks after Roberta returned and the cottage was filled with the sounds of life. John and the children were fascinated by the colors and lushness of Ireland and they loved listening to the Irish people tell stories about elementals. Roberta often found Deanne talking to the elementals when she thought no one was watching and took her aside one day to talk to her about this. Deanne explained that she had to be careful because the children at home made fun of her when she talked about seeing things they didn't see. Roberta assured her that she didn't have to be so careful about that here at the cottage because no one would make fun of her.

On a beautiful summer day shortly before the visit was to end, the entire family went for a picnic. After eating, the adults lazily stretched out on blankets under a large tree talking while the children played nearby. Roberta told them about her talk with Deanne, and the talk turned to the reservation. Both Tressa and John seemed very sad as they talked about how the people seemed to be turning away from their heritage and embracing the culture of those around them. They all watched as Deanne played and talked openly with the elementals, and John remarked how much happier she seemed here than at home.

They stayed for a month and when the day came for them to leave, Deanne clung to Roberta stating firmly that she wasn't leaving. Roberta held her close and whispered that she had to leave now but the time would come when she would be able to decide for herself where she wanted to live and until then she could visit every year. Her heart went out to this grandchild who shared her love of this magical place. Blair drove Tressa,

John and the children to the airport and everyone else said goodbye at
the cottage. Roberta waved until she could no longer see the little face
pressed against the rear window of the car and then entered the cottage.
She returned to sit outside in the warmth of the sun while she sipped a
cup of the tonic and let her thoughts wander.

After Tressa and her family left, Roberta rose early each morning to
bundle up and sit outside sipping tea while she painted hurriedly to catch
the special glow of early morning. She then put the painting aside and
enjoyed the chorus of the birds while she watched the elementals and earth
creatures as they scurried about.

On Sunday after everyone left, she went to church and joined some
of the other members for lunch. She made arrangements to help with
several projects and also signed up for a class once a week. It was early
evening when she returned home to find a light on and a small fire in the
fireplace. She walked over to thank Blair and Ruth and took them the copy
of Tressa's book she had brought from The States as a gift for them. She
told them about the volunteer work she was going to be doing and the
class she was to take. She kissed them each goodnight and thanked them
for their thoughtfulness.

She became caught up in the peace of the cottage and the beauty
surrounding her and felt a need to capture its many moods. On sunny
days, she would find a spot and paint until the chill drove her home. Her
favorite paintings were those of early morning, late afternoon or misty
days that seemed to be filled with mystery and magic. She often drove to a
distant area where she sketched scenes and later painted them with these
attributes. She kept her flute and lap harp with her to work on her music
after putting aside her paints or sketches. She also worked on her music
at night and hoped to have several good pieces to record by the time she
returned to The States in the fall.

Blair and Ruth sometimes joined Roberta when she went to church,
and Blair joined her a few times for the class, but he was reluctant to leave
Ruth alone as the time grew close for the baby to be born. Roberta often
took Sean with her on her drives to give Ruth a chance to rest. At first she
was nervous and constantly called him to her side, but then she realized
that the elementals were watching over him and relaxed her vigil. She did
several paintings of him playing with the elementals, which she showed to
Blair but not to Ruth for fear of upsetting her. Sean was a happy child and
seemed to thrive on being able to run freely and explore his world. He
would return after hours of play to cuddle with his head in her lap where
he promptly fell asleep while she played music.

Without Roberta being aware of it, she began to search for one
particular face at church. Trevor was often in the group when they went

to lunch after church, and he also attended the class. They had talked on numerous occasions, and he began to make it a point to sit beside her. They shared a love of art and music as well as their beliefs and could talk for hours without being bored. One Sunday when the group had gone to lunch, Trevor asked if he could come see some of her paintings, and Roberta invited him to dinner the following night. It was only when Blair teased her about her boyfriend that Roberta realized how much she enjoyed talking to Trevor and looked forward to seeing him again.

Trevor arrived just as the cottage was bathed in the last rays of the sun and stood as though lost in the moment. Roberta approached without a word, turned to look at her home and made a mental note to paint this scene. When the light faded, he handed her the flowers he had brought and they walked into the cottage together. The table was set before the fireplace where a small fire burned cheerfully, and Trevor helped as she put the food on the table. As they ate, he told her how beautiful the cottage was and how perfect a setting it seemed for her. Roberta had placed some of her paintings around the room, and they talked about them while they ate. When Trevor saw the painting of Sean playing with the elementals, he asked if she was able to see them and seemed envious when she said she could. She told him about the gnome that always came to comfort her when she was sad.

After dinner, Trevor insisted on helping with the dishes and then they sat by the fire sipping tea until 9 o'clock when he said he should get back to town. Roberta walked him out and waved as he drove away. She returned shivering to sit before the fire and stare into the flames and wonder where life was leading her. Once she had warmed up and the fire began to die down, she put on her gown and went to bed to lay awake thinking of Colin. Just as she was falling asleep, Colin appeared and told her he wanted her to be happy.

Wednesday night at class, Trevor invited Roberta to an outdoor concert on Saturday afternoon. Roberta accepted, and they arranged to meet in town for a late lunch before the concert. He had also suggested she bring Blair, Ruth and Sean but when she invited them the next day Ruth said she was too uncomfortable to sit for so long and Sean was too young to sit still. When they met Saturday, Roberta explained about Ruth and Sean and thanked him for including them. They had a light lunch and then made their way to a grassy knoll where he unfolded chairs for them. The concert was a mixture of Irish and light classical music.

After the concert, Roberta blushed when Trevor told her he had recognized one of her pieces. He told her then that he had bought as many of her recordings as he could find. They talked about the music over coffee and then Roberta drove home in the gathering darkness. The next day they had lunch with the group and after lunch Roberta gave Trevor a small painting she had done of the cottage at sunset the way it had been when he had been there.

Chapter 48

It was late July when Blair woke Roberta one night to stay with Sean while he took Ruth to the hospital to have the baby. Erin was born 18 hours later, let out one cry and calmly fell asleep sucking her fist. Ruth and Erin came home two days later and Roberta devoted all of her time to taking care of Ruth and the children for a couple of weeks. She was completely captivated by the tiny infant whose deep blue eyes were so like those of her grandfather Robert. After several weeks, when Ruth was recovered, Roberta returned to her routine taking Sean with her when she went to paint and play music. She had been so busy with the baby that there had been little time for Sean and she worried that he might be feeling neglected. He had constantly been told to be quiet so as not to wake the baby, but now he seemed to come alive as he romped and played with the elementals. Once he was completely worn out, he curled up as usual with his head on her lap and fell asleep as she played the flute.

The entire family went to church the next Sunday and Trevor sat beside Roberta. Except for several times that Trevor had come to dinner, she had not seen him since before Erin had been born. After church Trevor asked them to go for lunch but Ruth and the baby were tired, so he offered to drive Roberta home after lunch. It was still light when he brought her home, and he suggested they take a walk. Roberta led him to one of her favorite places on a rise overlooking the cottage and they sat together as shadows lengthened. The setting sun cast an eerie glow over the landscape and mist began to gather in patches lending an air of mystery to the landscape. They walked back to the cottage in silence and when Roberta turned to say goodnight Trevor bent to kiss her gently on the lips. She stood in the doorway long after the car disappeared from view savoring the kiss and thinking about Colin.

The following Wednesday night, after class, Roberta and Trevor sat in her car talking about the class for a while. When it was time to leave, Trevor took her in his arms and kissed her at first lightly and then with increasing passion as she responded in kind and then pulled away obviously shaken. Sensing that she was undergoing an internal battle, Trevor moved away slightly but kept his hand on her shoulder as he returned to casual conversation about the class, the baby, and everyday things. When the time came to leave, they said goodnight with a light, lingering kiss. That night Roberta lay awake torn between her love for Colin and her feelings for Trevor. Just as she drifted off to sleep, Colin appeared and told her it was time to let go of the past. As she slept, she dreamed of wandering the countryside with Colin as they had when they were young. She awoke knowing that she would always have these memories of the past and ready to embrace her future.

Roberta and Sean returned from one of their outings the following day to find Trevor visiting with Ruth and Erin while he waited for her to return. He apologized for arriving unannounced but said he had unexpectedly been invited to a party on Saturday night and wanted Roberta to go with him. Trevor helped Roberta carry everything into the house and then stood looking at the painting she had done that day of Sean playing with the elementals. Roberta invited Trevor to stay for dinner, and they talked about the painting while he helped her prepare a meal. They worked together cleaning up after dinner and then took a cup of tea to sit beside the fire and talk quietly. When they had finished their tea, Roberta rose, took Trevor's hand and led him to the spare bedroom. She went to her room to change and when she returned he was in bed waiting. He lifted the covers as she slipped between the sheets and into his arms. They made love in the light of a full moon that flooded the bed and then fell asleep. She awoke as his hands caressed her back and hips sending shivers of delight throughout her body once again.

The sun was high overhead when they had finally showered and dressed. They worked together to prepare a large breakfast often sharing a touch or kiss as they moved about the kitchen and then ate breakfast at the small table outside savoring the warm sunshine. After they had eaten, Roberta brought the lap harp out and played softly as they listened to the sounds of nature and the men working in the fields. They spent the rest of that day getting to know each other better and slept close together that night after making love. On Saturday morning they made arrangements to meet in town to attend the party that night, and she stood waving as he drove back to town.

She had met a few of the people at the party that night but most were strangers. As they circulated and Trevor introduced her, the talk was mostly of politics, conflicts around the world, economic problems and scandals. They had met at Trevor's place and after the party he invited her to stay the night, but she needed to go home in order to have something to wear to church the next day, so they said goodnight outside. As she drove home, she thought about the party and how heavy and dark the atmosphere had been. She had been surprised to find that Trevor was apparently completely comfortable, and she began to wonder if she knew him at all or if she was just too out of touch the world around her.

The next day, Ruth, Blair and the children joined her for church. She told them that she was going to drive her own car so that the family could leave whenever they wanted, and Blair winked as he mentioned having seen Trevor's car parked beside the cottage early Friday morning. Trevor sat with them as usual and surprised them all by inviting them to lunch at his home after church. The lunch was delicious and it was obvious that Trevor had spent a great deal of time preparing it. When Ruth commented on this, he explained he had always been interested in food and liked to experiment with different things.

After the family left, Roberta and Trevor sat on the front porch in the afternoon sunshine. Trevor's home was in a residential area where cars constantly passed and people occasionally walked by. As they watched the people passing, Roberta's thoughts turned again to the party. As though able to read her thoughts, Trevor asked how she had enjoyed the party, and Roberta hesitated trying to find a way to put her thoughts into words. It never occurred to Roberta to just lie and say she had enjoyed the party, and she finally told him it had been very interesting, but she had felt like an outsider because of the topics of conversation. Trevor was exposed to these things all of the time and had never thought much about it, and as they talked, he said that she lived a fairy tale life where nothing bad ever happened. Roberta pointed out that it is our perception of things that make them seem good or bad. He admitted that he found some of the things he heard at church hard to believe and they had a long talk about the seeming injustices in the world and karma and reincarnation. They ate the leftovers for dinner and then made love before she left to drive home.

She saw Trevor again at class on Wednesday night and invited him to dinner Friday night. After dinner Friday night as they sat sipping tea by the fire, she brought up the subject of her trip to The States and told him she would be leaving in a few weeks. She told him about her plans to visit Arizona and then make a new recording before returning to the clinic for the remainder of the winter. Trevor remarked that he had always wanted to visit The States but seemed surprised when she invited him to go with her and said he could and stay at the clinic with her. After talking it over for a few minutes, he said he had not taken a vacation for years and could take a full month off from work. He stayed until Saturday night and on Saturday he helped with some work around the cottage while they talked more about the trip. As they were working cleaning out flowerbeds, he said he had decided to go with her when she left for The States and stay as long as possible.

During the following weeks, Trevor stayed often at the cottage and Roberta showed him pictures of Arizona and the clinic. She loaned him Tressa's books to read in order for him to become acquainted with American Indian beliefs. She called Tressa and John to let them know that she would not be coming alone and make sure this would not cause a problem. They both assured her that it would not be a problem and they looked forward to meeting the man who had captured her heart. Her next call was to Francis to tell him about Trevor, and he was obviously happy to know that she was no longer alone.

When the time came to leave, Roberta was once again torn between reluctance to leave one part of her family and eagerness to see the other. Blair had offered to drive them to the airport and Trevor stayed over the night before they left to avoid him having to make extra stops. The family all had dinner together at the cottage and sat talking until time for bed. The next morning Roberta said goodbye to Ruth and the children with tears in her eyes and sat looking through the window at the cottage as they drove away. At the airport entrance, Blair helped unload the luggage, shook hands with Trevor and gave Roberta a hug and kiss before driving away.

Chapter 49

Francis met them when the plane landed, and Roberta introduced him to Trevor. She blushed as Francis kissed her on the cheek and whispered that love certainly seemed to agree with her. It was Saturday afternoon when they arrived at the clinic to find that a party had been arranged to welcome them. Tom and Judy were there as well as all who lived at the clinic and friends from church, and Carlan had managed to get away from school for the weekend. A large group of people surrounded Roberta, and Francis led Trevor to a quiet corner where they sat talking while Francis pointed out different people and introduced Trevor to those who came to meet him.

Trevor was fascinated by the work being done at the clinic and the lifestyle of those who lived there. He spent most of his time observing, asking questions and helping whenever he could while Roberta helped Sarah, Helena and Megan with the domestic chores and caught up on all of the news. Helena was pregnant and both Sarah and Megan hovered over her like mother hens lest she do something to harm herself or the baby. Helena confided to Roberta that she enjoyed the attention although she sometimes felt a little overwhelmed.

The following Wednesday Roberta and Trevor left for Arizona where they rented a car and drove to the reservation. As usual, John's family had arranged a large gathering to welcome them and meet Trevor. Tressa and John had arranged for them to stay on the reservation so that they didn't have to drive back and forth each day and would therefore have more time to spend with the family and still have privacy.

Roberta soon fell under the desert's spell. She rose early each morning and stopped what she was doing in the evening to try to capture the beauty of the sunrise and sunset in watercolors. Trevor was fascinated with the desert and shrugged off all warnings of its dangers until the day that he wandered off alone and had a close encounter with a rattlesnake. The snake struck and hit a sack he was carrying barely missing his leg. Having lived his life in Ireland, Trevor had no experience with snakes and was visibly shaken by the attack.

Roberta had noticed that Tressa seemed less involved in things on the reservation than in the past and one day when they were alone she brought this up. Tressa said that the things she had helped get for the reservation no longer needed her, and she confined herself to working with the elders to preserve the heritage of the tribe. She said that despite everything the elders tried to do the reservation was steeped in an attitude of poverty and despair and she and John had talked about leaving the reservation for the sake of the children. Roberta commented on the difference she had noticed in Deanne here compared to when she was in Ireland. Tressa told Roberta that John and the children had all loved Ireland and they had toyed with the idea of moving there. Roberta suggested that they live on the farm in the summer to help Blair and live on the reservation in the winter until they knew for sure what they wanted to do. Tressa could do her research for her books during the winter and then write in the summer in Ireland. As they talked, Roberta saw the excitement grow in Tressa's eyes and that night at dinner she told the family what Roberta had suggested. Roberta watched Deanne and saw the little girl seem to come to life at the thought of living part of the year in Ireland.

The visit soon came to an end but everyone waved goodbye with smiles as the old truck bounced over the rough roads toward the airport because plans had been made for Tressa, John and the children to come to the clinic for Christmas and to spend most of the next summer in Ireland.

Frances was waiting when they reached the airport, and on the way back to the clinic, they talked about Tressa and her family and their plan to spend the following summer in Ireland. Dinner that evening was a noisy, cheerful gathering that reminded Roberta of her childhood and later as she, Trevor, Frances and Megan sat on the porch she and Francis reminisced about their life at the center. Neither Trevor nor Megan saw the family and those who had lived at the center appear briefly in the moonlight.

Roberta and Trevor joined in helping at the clinic during the day. She had made arrangements to meet with Troy and Dorian to practice and choose the pieces they would record, and Trevor insisted she not change her plans because he enjoyed listening to them play. They met at the pub four nights each week often accompanied by others from the clinic.

The night before Trevor was to leave, he told Roberta he envied her the magic she and her family seemed to have in their lives. As they lay talking,

Anna and Robert appeared in the shaft of moonlight that fell across the bed. Trevor sat in stunned silence as they talked about the wonders of life and what lay beyond this world. When they faded from view, Roberta explained matter-of-factly that he had just met her mother and father.

After Trevor left, Roberta contacted Mr. Blake and made arrangements to meet for the first recording session in one week. She, Troy and Dorian had chosen most of the pieces they would record and spent most of their time fine-tuning those pieces. Helena surprised Roberta one night when she said she had written lyrics for one of the pieces and asked if she could sing with them. The piece was one of Roberta's favorites that she had written one foggy morning when she had been missing Colin more than usual. When Helena began to sing, a hush fell over the pub and at the end of the piece there was thunderous applause. After that, Helena wrote lyrics for another of the pieces and joined them by either playing or singing whenever they practiced. Helena also joined them when they made the recordings, and Mr. Blake was astonished when it only took three days to finish them.

Life at the clinic was busy with the holidays and Tressa, John and the children visiting at Christmas, and soon a new year was beginning. Carlan was at the clinic for a couple of weeks at Christmas and told Roberta he had been dating a young woman at school. As he talked about the girl and his studies, Roberta silently offered a prayer of thanksgiving. He would be finishing his studies in the summer and planned to return to the clinic to work.

That winter was unusually cold and as the weather grew colder, Roberta's arthritis became more painful despite the tonic that Francis mixed for her and energy healings she received. She continued to work in the clinic and do some painting but found it difficult at times to hold the brushes or to play the harp.

Spring came at last and everything seemed to be celebrating as flowers burst forth seemingly overnight and tree branches groaned under an abundance of blossoms and new leaves. Roberta often sat on the porch letting the sun warm her painful joints. As she sat sipping a cup of tea one day, she became aware that something within her seemed to have slowed. As she pondered this, the gnome appeared beside her, and she asked if he knew what this meant. The gnome explained that just as the animals and plants know when a season is ending the body knows when its time is coming to a close and responds by slowing down. When he saw the alarm on Roberta's face, he hurried to assure her that it didn't mean she was going to die right away, but rather she was entering the final phase of life in preparation for that passing. He told her that this allowed for an easier passing than if one were rushing about and then suddenly passed, rather like the difference between a car suddenly slamming into a wall at high speed or coming slowly to a gentle stop. Roberta thought about all of the people she knew who had passed and realized that most had gone through a slowing down period before death. As she looked around the room that night, she became aware of the slower movement of the older members of the family. She saw each of them in a new light and when she looked at Francis she saw how stooped he was and how slowly he moved and realized that his time must be quite near. Her heart ached as she thought about losing her beloved brother until she reminded herself that he would not be lost and she would soon be with him.

Chapter 50

Roberta returned to Ireland in May and as usual her heart swelled with love at the sight of her little cottage. Tressa and her family arrived a few days after Roberta. Each of them soon settled into their own rhythm and the cottage was once again filled with the energy of the young. At times, Roberta longed for peace and quiet but when everyone was out she realized how lonely it was and was happy to see them all again. She saw Trevor quite often and occasionally stayed overnight with him. They enjoyed each other's company and could talk for hours on many subjects. He had mentioned marriage once, but Roberta said she preferred things the way they were and he never mentioned it again.

In September Tressa and her family left for Arizona and Roberta made her plans to leave in October for the clinic looking forward to the warmer climate. She was relieved not to be going to Arizona this year because travel was not the joy it had once been. Trevor stayed with her the night before she left and took her to the airport the next day. He had talked about possibly coming for a visit during the holidays but nothing was definite.

Trevor did visit the clinic for two weeks between Thanksgiving and Christmas and Tressa, John and the children came for two weeks at Christmas. Carlan was working at the clinic and surprised everyone by inviting his girlfriend to visit and announcing their engagement. Helena had given birth to a son in June and already had another on the way, so building was taking place to accommodate the increasing family.

Francis passed away quietly in his sleep two weeks after Christmas, was laid to rest beside Anna and Robert, and the family consoled each other and grieved each in their own way. Roberta and Megan sat on the porch one spring night shortly before Roberta was to return to Ireland talking about all the years they had known each other and the things they had shared. The passing of Francis had left each of them with a hole in their life that nothing could fill, and Megan said she was thinking of going back to Ireland with Roberta for a visit.

Roberta and Megan returned to Ireland in May and were met at the airport by Blair and Maureen. Megan was to stay with Maureen at the family home, so they said goodbye at the airport. As Roberta hugged Megan and kissed her cheek, she knew that she was saying a final goodbye in this world.

Tressa, John and the children arrived in June and the cottage once again hummed with life. John worked on the farm while Tressa wrote and Roberta painted and played music. Deanne began to show an interest in the paints and Roberta furnished her supplies and encouraged her. Roberta seldom went far from the house now, so her subject matter was limited. Deanne often went exploring alone and kept a camera with her. She had a good eye for composition, and Roberta began to use some of her pictures as subjects for her paintings. Jonathon seemed content to work with his father and uncle on the farm.

As usual Tressa, John and the children left in September for Arizona and Roberta prepared for her own trip in October. Traveling was becoming more difficult because of having to sit for such a long time, and she wondered how much longer she would be able to make the trip.

Chapter 51

For the next two years, Roberta's life followed the established routine of winters at the clinic and summers in Ireland. Carlan married Sandra, the girl he had met at school, the first week in December, and they moved into their own cabin at the clinic. Tressa, John and their children came for the wedding and stayed until after Christmas. Carlan and Sandra's daughter Janine was born in January the following year.

Tressa and John left the reservation and settled permanently in Ireland the year that Janine was born, and a small apartment was added to the cottage for Roberta so she could have a private place of her own when she returned in the spring.

The third year, Roberta decided that she could no longer make the trips back and forth and decided to stay in Ireland. She was taking an arthritis medication that Carlan had told her about and it seemed to help, and her apartment had a good heating system that cut down on the dampness so the winters were easier for her. Though she would miss those at the clinic, without Francis and Megan, Roberta felt old and out of place among all of the young people and their children even though they always made her feel welcome.

On a bright spring day four years later Roberta sat drinking a cup of hot tea. She placed the cup on the table beside the chair and leaned back closing her eyes. The room was suddenly filled with a bright light, and she saw Colin walking toward her with his arms open. Her mother, father, Francis, Diana, and Aunt Lillith stood behind Colin as though waiting for her, and Roberta felt young and light as she ran to meet them. At first she was confused, but as she turned and saw the old lady sitting slumped in the chair she realized she had made the feared transition from life into death. As they rose up and out of the cottage, she looked back on her magical cottage and her beloved Ireland with a smile.

It was Tressa who found her mother a few hours later when she came to see if Roberta wanted to join them for supper or just have a tray in her room. As she sank to her knees beside the chair, her thoughts went back to the days when her father had been missing and it was just the two of them. The memories of all the years since flooded through her as tears flowed unchecked down her cheeks. After giving herself some time alone to grieve and say goodbye, she finally rose to go tell the others and saw, through tear filled eyes, her mother and father standing young and healthy in the shaft of light coming in the window.

Roberta was laid to rest beside Colin at his family home. As the cars drove away from the family home, Tressa saw her father and mother standing with her grandparents at the landing window. Carlan, Sandra and Helena had come for the funeral and planned to stay for a few days before returning to the States, and that night they all gathered in the cottage to go through and divide the pictures and personal items of Roberta and Colin. Each item brought forth memories of their childhood and tears flowed freely as they sat surrounded by the memories of a lifetime.

Printed in the United States
95452LV00002B/525/A

9 781425 735852